Dawn's Light in Monterey

Dawn's Light in Monterey

Women of Monterey, Book 2

Marilyn Read
Cheryl Spears Waugh

For information:
Tranquility Press
723 W University Ave #300-234
Georgetown TX 78626
TranquilityPress.Net
TranquilityPress@gmail.com

Cover design: Ken Raney, KenRaney.com

ISBN: 978-1-950481-02-6
PCN: 2019935624

Publisher's Cataloging-in-Publication data

Names: Read, Marilyn, author. | Waugh, Cheryl Spears, author.
Title: Dawn's light in Monterey / by Marilyn Read and Cheryl Spears Waugh.
Series: Women of Monterey.
Description: Georgetown, TX: Tranquility Press, 2019.
Identifiers: LCCN 2019935624 |
ISBN 978-1-950481-02-6 (paperback) | ISBN 978-1-950481-05-7 (e-Book)
Subjects: LCSH Mission San Carlos Borromeo (Carmel, Calif.)--History--Fiction. | Franciscans--Missions--California--History--Fiction. | Missions, Spanish--California--History--Fiction. | Indians of North America--Missions--California--History--Fiction. | Healers--Fiction. | Sisters--Fiction. | Man-woman relationships--Fiction. | Family--Fiction. | Love stories. | BISAC FICTION / Historical / General

Classification: LCC PS3618.E2242 D39 2019 | DDC 813.6--dc23

To the next generation of strong women:

Jordan, Carlee, Jolee, and Brynlee.

May you love God with all your heart,
trusting Him for today and tomorrow.

One

Rancho de Montaraz, June 1807

Casa de Montaraz! The domain of Don León de Montaraz, once the most powerful rancher in Monterey. People spoke in awe of the dwelling and of its master. He'd passed on, but his cattle empire thrived in the hands of his four aristocratic sons.

Aurora Rivera sat in Fray Peralta's small open carriage outside the front gate. Time felt like it was slowing down as she tried to quell the fluttery feeling in her stomach. Was it curiosity—or foreboding?

A curving drive stretched before her, leading to an immense house. If only Pía were beside her, she'd welcome the adventure of finding what lay beyond. But her sister was far down the coast battling an epidemic.

By following Fray Peralta's insightful advice five years earlier, Pía had developed her nursing ability and become a valued citizen of the province. She now traveled with a soldier guard because of her importance. Her keen diagnostic powers and her success with native remedies had put her in demand when illness struck on the big ranches and even at other missions.

Now it was Aurora's turn to consider the extraordinary foresight of Fray Peralta. At twenty-two, she was too mature to be wavering on such a life-changing decision, but her mission work seemed more important than whatever she could accomplish on this ranch. She bit her lower lip until it hurt.

God often led his followers into uncertainty. The choice was hers. Set aside her familiar life as a respected teacher in the mission classroom and take on a new identity, albeit a more humble one. The idea was intriguing. The very loss of status made her think it was of God. He honored humility.

"Well, my daughter-in-Christ?" Fray Peralta's steady blue gaze searched her face.

"You feel certain God calls me here?"

"I am convinced, Aurora, and I pray you will be also." The friar paused as his keen eyes searched her face. "Your name means *Dawn.* A new day. At your birth, Fray Serra suggested it to your parents. Perhaps your coming signals new blessings for the people of this ranch."

Aurora's eyebrows lifted. "I can only hope for such an outcome, but you were certainly right in your advice to Pía. She says she would have missed her calling had you not encouraged her to stay at the mission instead of going into a convent."

"She has become a nurse of renown. God uses her talents for the good of many. It was his plan, not mine."

"Just as He uses me for the good of many children at the mission. Yet you say God's call for me to come to this ranch is as clear to you as God's call for Pía."

Fray Peralta's response was a solemn nod.

Blinking rapidly, Aurora chose her next words carefully. "Both Mamá and Papá were in service here. He was the *caporal* for many years. Yet he left to care for the smaller herds of the mission. He never told me why."

Unease clung to her skin like a film of oil. Papá was a loyal man. *Caporal* meant he was second-in-command of this vast holding. Something must have gone terribly wrong if he left his long-standing position.

She studied the friar's face. "Once Papá's reason seemed unimportant. I never imagined myself at the ranch. But now it feels like a mystery I need to solve before I accept service here."

Fray Peralta did not respond, instead reaching down for his water flask, averting his gaze as he drank.

Aurora prodded, "I wish now I had asked more questions, but I never thought..." Her jaw set and she pushed her shoulders back. One more try. "Can you can enlighten me, Father?"

The friar's expression retained its usual benevolence. He took a long draw on his water flask and patted her hand. "Mother Anna and daughter Aurora: both lovely women of courage, master teachers with hearts for God and a thirst for answers."

She tilted her chin down and frowned. Soothing, but not helpful. If there was some compelling reason why her parents left Rancho de Montaraz, the friar was not prepared to tell her. She would have to discover for herself.

A memory flashed up—a strange occurrence she hadn't thought of for years. Present surroundings faded as the sights and sounds of a long-ago morning rushed back to her.

Ten or eleven years ago—not long before Papá's death—she and Pía strolled with him around the quadrangle of Mission San Carlos at Monterey when a well-dressed stranger rode through the gate.

He stood in his stirrups and looked intently at them. The moment lengthened and Papa's face changed. He looked drawn and preoccupied. If she hadn't known better, Aurora might have thought he was frightened. Something seemed to pass between the men and Papá returned to normal, taking Aurora's hand.

The girls had plied Papá with questions: Who was the elegant man, astride a prancing black stallion? Why had he stared at them?

"Don León de Montaraz," Papá replied, nodding in the don's direction.

Aurora remembered bouncing on her toes. At last she would meet the mysterious rancher! She'd never before seen him at the mission, but her friends spoke of him. They said Don and Doña de Montaraz sent gifts of fruit and small coins for the mission orphans at Christmas, and that even the Presidente of all California missions, Father Lasúen, went to Rancho de Montaraz when Don León sent word.

Surely he'd want to talk with Papá. They'd worked closely together for many years. Perhaps he would also want to see Mamá, since she had served his wife.

Don León de Montaraz dismounted, withdrew a book from his saddlebag, and entered the open doors of the imposing mission without a second look in their direction.

"A busy man," Papá had explained.

More than likely Don León was like Aurora's uncle. Aristocrats worshiped money and power. People with little social standing held no interest for them.

Mamá's patrician brother, Porfirio, proved that. He'd squandered her inheritance and ruined her plans for an important marriage after the death of their parents. Then he'd sent Mamá into the world with a single gold coin to sustain her. Long accustomed to a grand life, she had to work as a servant in the household of Don León.

Mamá said the story held a lesson for Aurora and her younger sister. "God had a far better plan for my life than mine. He led me to Papá and into a life filled with joy and purpose," she had said.

Aurora might now be surrounded by the four aristocratic sons of the deceased Don León de Montaraz. The eldest son, Don Iván, had offered her a position as a governess and teacher for his young daughter.

Fray Peralta's summation of the brothers had not been reassuring. "Men of lusty appetites for life, who present a united front to the world."

Would they take her seriously? Her teaching methods, learned at Mamá's side in the mission school, were unconventional. Success required shared confidence and esteem between teacher, pupil, and parent. Could a servant gain the respect of aristocrats? It would be a challenge.

She never shrank from challenge if she felt God's push to try. She'd grown up with the story of Father Junípero Serra, who had walked from Mexico City to California on a damaged foot in peasant's sandals. He'd had only God's vision to guide him. The result was a string of flourishing missions on the coast and thousands of converts.

Aurora couldn't yet see God's purpose for her at Rancho de Montaraz, but she trusted Fray Peralta's wisdom. He loved her as his daughter-in-Christ and he heard God's voice clearly. She felt compelled to investigate. She murmured words Papá had often spoken to her. "*Tomo prestado problemas*."

Fray Peralta chuckled. "You admit you're borrowing trouble? Are you willing to set aside your misgivings and proceed?"

"I don't yet see what I can possibly accomplish here, a simple woman surrounded by four aristocratic men, but you say God calls me. Something inside me agrees and I feel I must try."

Like Mamá's story, her own had become a departure from her expectations. Once through that gateway, her life would change, perhaps irrevocably. Was she truly prepared to sacrifice her heart's satisfaction of teaching many children in the mission classroom for tutoring only Jocasta, the daughter of an aristocrat? Aurora sighed, shamed by her prejudice.

Her maternal grandfather, Rodrigo Arista, had been a godly man, generous and caring, though a Spanish aristocrat. But she could not imagine him building a house like the one shaded by trees of an extensive garden. Palatial. That was the word. She had never seen anything like it.

Fray Peralta pointed up at the arching gateway above them. "Notice the curious rocks. Some of them came from great distances, chosen by Don León for their uniqueness."

"Yes, Father, the gateway is impressive, but I never imagined a house of this size and grandeur." She pursed her lips. "It's late to ask, but seeing this house makes me wonder. Is my employer a spiritual man? Do we at least have that in common?"

The friar remained silent for several moments. "I wish I knew. Don Iván does not speak of his beliefs. His mother was devout and tried to instill her faith in her sons, but the eldest was close to his father. Don León did not consult me in matters of faith. In his lifetime he spoke only to the *Presidente* of the missions. To my knowledge Don Iván confers with no one."

Aurora's hand sought her mother's crucifix at her throat—the one Grandfather Rodrigo had given her as a reminder that God is always near.

As the carriage moved forward, the house revealed more of its splendor. Local clay used in the adobe was rich brown, a perfect foil for the tiled roof supported by carved timber corbels. Curved tiles lay in a complex symmetry of reddish orange, tan, and pale yellow.

"How many rooms, Father?"

"Possibly as many as one hundred. I've been in only the public spaces, but servants live in the house, as well as the family. And in Don León's time many guests and travelers."

So engrossed was she in the sight before her that he sounded far away. Aurora shook her head.

"Far too much. Why would anyone construct such a grand house?"

A slight smile tipped the friar's lips, but he answered seriously enough.

"Only God knows. I've become accustomed to imposing structures after the new Mission San Carlos de Borromeo was completed ten years ago. Some consider it the most beautiful in all of California."

"Yes, but the mission is purposed in glory to God and used by a thousand people. Only a few live here. So unlike the way of the friars and my parents..."

Aurora felt her cheeks heat and drew a breath. "Forgive me, Father. I must not criticize." She really must not. It was not a good beginning.

"Yes, wait and see, my child. Learn the facts before you form an opinion." Friar Peralta softened his words with another pat to her hand and urged the horse along the circular drive. "The hacienda is a vast enterprise, as I'm sure you noted on the road here, with its hemp factory, and large herds of sheep and cattle. It employs many people, Aurora. Scores of lives are enriched."

The breeze carried a scent of damp earth and of the many plants surrounding her. Tears shimmered as Aurora remembered the pleasures of helping her pupils learn the names of trees and flowers in the mission gardens.

Now there would be only one little girl, a child of privilege. Could she motivate her to see God's grace amid the luxury that surrounded her?

Aurora's chest tightened. Could she ever feel at home in this monument to wealth? She closed her eyes for a moment before reaching for Friar Peralta's arm, then stepped from the carriage onto the deep veranda.

Washed in a golden ocher, its walls offered a pleasing contrast to the dark brown of the rest of the house. Its quarry-tiled floor held a few puddles from a recent washing. Leather-covered tables and chairs interspersed its length, and flowering baskets hung from overhead beams. Water gurgling in a nearby fountain lent cool tranquility on a hot day.

At Fray Peralta's first rap of the iron knocker, a graying man in rancher's attire opened the double entry doors and stood back, beaming.

The friar embraced him. "Jorge, you old rascal, I've struggled to forgive you for abandoning me for the trappings of society. Don Iván said he'd expect us at this hour."

Aurora looked around and gasped. She'd stepped into a ballet of rainbows! Mid-afternoon light poured in and bounced off polished floor tiles and golden walls. Large transom windows set far above the massive doors and sheltering porch created the magic. The colors shifted, merged, and separated, as though alive.

A two-story space came into focus as her eyes adjusted to the dazzling display. Enchantment faded. Another reminder of the prosperity and taste of Don León de Montaraz.

Two staircases swept upward at either side, guarded by scrolled wrought iron railings that ran across an upper landing.

Aurora glimpsed doors and hallways on both levels. Detail after sumptuous detail bombarded her. Pía told stories of the elegant houses she'd worked in, but never anything like this. How would she find her way around?

"Don Iván awaits you in his office. His brothers are at work, but he waited to welcome you."

Jorge led the way through an archway into a small anteroom. Several niches contained *santos.* One of the carved saint figures, gaunt and arresting, caught Aurora's attention and she paused before it.

"The melding of two cultures, Aurora," Fray Peralta murmured. "Carvings in the house are the work of some of our mission artisans. Don León paid them handsomely for their work."

Jorge knocked on one of the double doors.

"*Adelante*. Enter."

Aurora's throat tightened. The deep voice was that of a man accustomed to unquestioning obedience.

Two

Aurora stepped through the office door and stopped short. A man rose from behind a massive desk on the left, many feet away. Even the arched stained-glass window soaring behind him and the length of the office could not dwarf his height or his powerful build. He had to be six feet tall. His outline was only a silhouette, but his straight stance and wide shoulders were impressive.

Her hand went to her crucifix. He strode toward her with the grace of a panther. As he neared, his gaze riveted on her. A wild creature advancing on its prey.

His clean-shaven face was dark with a strong, square jawline. Lengthy, slightly unruly hair hung from a center part in loose, black waves. Covering his ears, it brushed the tops of his broad shoulders, thick and vibrant.

Montaraz. Untamed. A fitting name.

As if sensing her thoughts, Fray Peralta placed her hand on his arm, and led her forward to meet her new employer.

"Don Iván de Montaraz, it is my pleasure to present to you Señorita Aurora Rivera-Arista. Señorita Rivera is the young lady of whom we spoke when you came to me two weeks ago."

Don Iván stood staring at her, an intriguing expression on his face. She tried to read what she saw, but it was difficult. Surprise? No, more like shock. Why?

His expression cleared, and he bowed over the hand held in his large, dark one. His lips brushed lightly along its top and Aurora felt her color rise. It would be a cold female soul not charmed by such a gesture from this man.

Don Iván greeted her in the formal Castilian manner. "At your service, Señorita Rivera. I am most grateful to you for coming to my aid. When I appealed to Fray Peralta, he offered reassurances about your abilities."

The words welcomed, but his black eyes, as shiny as mirrors, appeared guarded. His voice was deep and confident, but not particularly warm. No smile. *Concise, formal. An aristocrat to his toes.*

Friar Peralta's description placed her employer as nearing thirty years of age, a widower with a young daughter who suffered a visual disability. Don Iván dressed as most *hacendados,* the gentleman ranchers of New Spain. A loose, snowy-white linen shirt showed beneath a silver-ornamented, short black leather vest.

Her unwilling glance revealed black leather trousers encasing his long, muscular legs. The sides of the tight breeches were fastened with silver buttons from ankle to loin, and flat-heeled black leather boots, gleaming like onyx, peeped from their unbuttoned hemlines. A scarlet sash around his waist provided a single touch of color.

Aurora looked up into the inscrutable face of Don Iván de Montaraz and felt her cheeks heat. He must have caught her appraisal of his physical attributes. Chiseled face, straight nose, long mouth. Not handsome by ordinary standards, yet possibly the finest-looking man she had ever seen.

A stillness about him struck her. He stood composed and quiet, the essence of power controlled. What was he thinking?

She spoke without smiling. Everything about the man required gravity. "Thank you for your welcome, Señor de Montaraz. I am astounded by the splendor of your home, and look forward to meeting your daughter."

The sound of her voice commanded a second, surprised glance. Her clear, husky voice, the voice of her mother, was unexpected, coming from such a small woman. Men seemed to react to it.

"Friar Peralta tells me she is four years old. I have worked with young children at the mission school."

"I can only hope your experience will have prepared you for dealing with my Jocasta."

Rueful smile; even, white teeth.

He continued, "She is by some standards considered to be a handful. I love her more than my life, but I must recognize she can be willful."

Surely not beyond your control. Nothing would be.

"I believe she will respond to your charm, however, Señorita Rivera." He gestured. "Please, let us be seated and enjoy refreshment."

He led the way to one of several small tables flanked by armchairs. Without effort he lifted a third to jostle for space, extending the gateleg to accommodate his guests. Jorge appeared on cue with a silver coffee service and slices of a rich-looking cake.

After she was seated and the coffee poured, Aurora cast a peek at Don Iván. He studied his cup in silence. She decided to pick up the conversation in response to his comment about charm.

"Señor de Montaraz, I am not sure charm will be helpful in dealing with Jocasta—"

Iván de Montaraz raised his head, his eyes narrowed.

Aurora closed her own and pressed back into her chair. *Let me finish.* Formidable, his protectiveness.

She regained control. "But caring and patience often are. I will take time to discover her interests and her personality." She forced herself to meet his gaze.

His head cocked. The fathomless scrutiny absorbed her, as if time did not matter to him.

How could he so quickly push her off balance? It wasn't a feeling to which she was accustomed. Aurora sat still under his examination and kept her voice steady.

"Patience develops with determining personality. I love children. I was well-loved by two godly parents, so I understand nurture. God has prepared me for His call to care for the young. I take little credit."

Don Iván's dark face remained unreadable, his wrists resting on the table in the accepted Spanish manner. Aurora steeled herself to return his cool, measuring look and was gratified at last to recognize what she hoped was a tiny glow of warmth.

"A statement filled with wisdom, I believe. I am hopeful things will work out." He ran a hand through his unruly hair.

He couldn't be nervous. He wouldn't know the meaning of the word.

"You can set your terms of employment, Señorita, including hours away from your duties. Jocasta has an attendant, Luisa, who tends to her personal needs. My daughter is used to the run of the house, except for the stairs. She loves the gardens and never lacks for caretakers among house servants and gardeners. I spend as much time with her as possible and my three brothers are her slaves, so you will have help always at hand." His face softened as he spoke of his child.

Jocasta could well be a handful with a houseful of admirers dancing attendance. Aurora looked at Fray Peralta and managed a wobbly smile. How she would miss him.

"My few worldly goods came with us. Fray Peralta was amazingly certain of my acceptance even before our interview."

Don Iván turned toward the padre with a glance that held an obvious wordless communication. Fray Peralta nodded.

Aurora frowned. What was the shared understanding between them? She sought the friar's attention, but his expression revealed only its usual goodwill.

Breaking a lengthy silence, she said, "I assume I will have a room near that of Jocasta. Fray Peralta has allowed me to bring some of my teaching materials from the mission. Is there a space we can use as a schoolroom?"

"*Sí, Señorita*. You have a well-appointed bedroom and study adjoining Jocasta's. A large nursery completes my daughter's suite and can serve as a school room. It has a few books. Enjoy full use of the extensive library in this office, as well."

Jorge approached and refilled the men's cups after Aurora placed her palm over her own.

Don Iván paused, cup half-way to his lips. "Jocasta needs the influence of a cultured woman and the discipline of a classroom and proper studies. All she knows is this ranch and male attitudes." He studied Aurora, once again unperturbed by the passing seconds.

She looked to Fray Peralta. He smiled and nodded, as if pleased with the proceedings.

Iván de Montaraz called her attention back to him. "You have only to ask for what you need. If there is anything lacking—anything for you or for the schoolroom—please feel free to mention it, and it will be obtained. Through the port we can acquire the goods of the world, although some take time."

He could not be serious. Anything she wanted?

"I am sure Friar Peralta has explained my daughter's visual disability. An accident on the stairs damaged her eyesight, but she is bright and has adapted. She is rather fearless in a world she cannot see well."

Real smile. Proud, protective father; willful child; slavish uncles—we shall see.

"María will be your personal maid. She is also a skilled dressmaker, who was in service to my mother. Jorge will bring her to show you to your room and explain the layout of the house."

A lady's maid for a paid servant?

"You may take the rest of the day to settle. Tomorrow perhaps you will be ready to begin your work with Jocasta. She is riding with my brothers this afternoon. You will meet them at dinner tonight. We expect you to dine with the family each morning and evening."

His request held all the force of insistence without being blatant. What could she say? Surprising to be asked—no, commanded—to dine with the family, but his offer to obtain anything she wanted took her breath away.

To have such wealth seemed impossible. Friars had to account for every piece of hardware they requested from Mexico City. Her teaching tools were limited to ones she made.

With a dismissive nod, Don Iván turned to Friar Peralta. "Will you take the evening meal with us?"

"No, I will return to work." Fray Peralta arose and the others with him. He embraced Aurora. "Let us part with a prayer."

The exchange between Don Iván and Aurora had gone well. Her spirit and her natural dignity well displayed. Her departure would leave a hole in his life, but he was aging and wanted to see her settled into a more stable life than that of the mission. It would have been the wish of his mentor, Fray Serra, a personal friend of Aurora's mother, and of her grandfather, Rodrigo.

The importance of missions would decrease with a changing political landscape. Their future was uncertain. Responding to internal decay of the Spanish Empire, the last two kings of Spain had weakened the church and its monasteries and missions.

Casa de Montaraz offered great possibility to

Aurora, depending upon many factors, all of which were out of his hands—but not out of the hands of God.

If only he could have prepared her for the situation she faced, but he was bound by the rules of the confessional and the wishes of Don Iván to reveal nothing of the true story. He could not speak of Don León, Aurora's actual father, the adoption of his sons, or the actual reason for her summons.

I advised him truth was the way. Her appearance had to be a shock for him.

Fray Peralta breathed a prayer of petition for her well-being in the hacienda with its four strong men and one headstrong little girl. God would have His loving hands full, and so would Aurora.

Fray Peralta traced the sign of the cross onto Aurora's upturned forehead and whispered, "*Amar a Dios*. Love God. Seek God Himself. To know Him, to resemble Him, and to delight in Him, my child, and allow Him to delight in you. For this you were created. Look forward—never back."

The friar's throat tightened as he watched a tear roll down Aurora's cheek. He waited, but Don Iván did not invite a blessing. Adjusting his cowl, Fray Peralta stepped toward the door, then paused.

He turned and challenged Don Iván with a look. Responsibility was all on the don's broad shoulders now. In the black eyes regarding him, the padre found no reassurance.

Jorge brought her trunk; María arrived; and Aurora followed the servants out the doorway. Iván de Montaraz watched her graceful progress across the floor, half expecting her to look back at him. She did not.

Raking a hand through his hair, he turned to his desk. One glance assured him he had no appetite for the work, and he reached for a decanter of brandy on the desk's corner. His hand halted.

He turned away and paced the floor. Finally, he leaned against the mantel, staring into the remnants of the morning's small fire.

Not what he'd expected. She was far too beautiful. Surprisingly poised and spirited. Without flinching, she'd met his most intimidating gaze—the one that could quell even Raúl. How would his brothers react? Her resemblance to Father was astounding. The widow's peak, chestnut hair, and arresting gray-green eyes.

Father charged me with preserving unity between his sons, but I may have unwittingly driven a wedge between us.

Iván shrugged. Fray Peralta advised truth from the start, but truth would not serve in this situation. He could always reign in matters if they threatened to move beyond his control. He managed his strong-willed brothers and countless ranch employees. Surely one young woman could offer no threat to his peace of mind.

Three

Aurora's hand wavered above the stair railing and her foot hesitated to mount the first step. Jorge was far above, her trunk bumping along behind him.

"This way, Señorita," Maria said. "I will assist you with anything you need."

Into Your hands, Holy Father. The prayer Mamá offered whenever circumstances were uncertain—the one Grandfather Rodrigo said never failed. Up the steps into her new life.

"Are there adult female family members in the house?"

María paused on the step above and shook her head. "No grandmothers or aging aunts. Luisa and I will be your *chaperonas*."

Aurora pressed her lips together. Two busy women would not have time for confidences. Fray Peralta was at the mission four miles distant and Pía was far away. The ache in her heart increased.

María reached the top and waited as Jorge passed Aurora on his way down the stairs. She said, "I remember your mother, Señorita Aurora. She was kind to a young servant frightened by her responsibilities. Ramona, our former cook, and your mother were great friends."

Aurora smiled. "Mamá loved Ramona. I remember how sad she was at her funeral." She paused for a look around. "It must take a large staff to operate this house."

María stood aside for Aurora to enter the room she indicated.

"Besides Jorge, who acts as *mayor domo* and valet to Don Iván, there are four personal domestics who care for the brothers and Jocasta. We have a number of general housemaids and footmen, a soap maker, and a butter-and-cheese man. He milks from fifty to sixty cows every day with a little help."

She crossed to Aurora's trunk, opened the lid, then eased it closed again. "Shall we tour the house before I unpack?"

The plan suited Aurora. "Do you remember which was my mother's room?"

"The house has been rebuilt since her time. Much larger than when she was here. Don Iván's three brothers have downstairs rooms. Don Iván, of course, uses his parents' apartment upstairs. His rooms, yours, and Jocasta'a share the long balcony over the front porch."

The tour revealed elaborate family rooms, servant quarters, and several kitchens: a seasonal canning kitchen, one for meal preparation, and a bakery. Sofía, the head cook, and a flock of assistants greeted them.

Gesturing from a kitchen door, María pointed out a vegetable garden and the door to a large ice cellar protecting perishables. Beyond lay a number of dependencies.

"A great many servants, María."

She laughed. "Oh, many more than I mentioned. Four washer women and three to iron, two errand boys, one shoemaker, and a dressmaker—me. Three gardeners. A vintner and distiller, and now a governess."

"I cannot begin to calculate the expense of maintaining such a staff," Aurora said.

Everything on the hacienda was dedicated to maintaining a pattern of cultured living for discriminating people in exile. A recreation of the aristocratic life of old Spain in a new land. Comfort, comfort, comfort.

Aurora thought of the simple lives the friars led. Each had one room containing a narrow cot, a shelf, and a table and chair. Managing this enormous house and hacienda must be a weighty responsibility.

"Shall I finish the list, Señorita?" María's eyes twinkled as Aurora's widened.

"Really? There are more?"

"I sometimes put myself to sleep reciting the list. Four wool combers, two carpenters and a plasterer. A saddle maker, two tanners, and a harness maker. A blacksmith and his helper. The *estableros*: a stable manager and several grooms. Six shepherds and two swineherds. A miller who operates the grist mill on the river, and a canal manager and three laborers who keep water flowing to house, fields, and gardens."

She paused and Aurora laughed at the game.

"Three machinists and numerous employees who operate the factory that processes rope fibers. Then, of course, the many *vaqueros*."

"And now you're out of breath." They giggled together.

On her outside tour María pointed out a harness shop, a blacksmith shop, a carpenter shop, a saddlery, a gardeners' house, and the head cook's cottage. Near the vineyards stood a winepress and a fermentation room, with quarters nearby for the vintner and distiller. No mention was made of the *matadero,* which Aurora assumed would be hidden behind a hill, well away from the main house. Every ranch had a slaughter house.

The mission also operated many enterprises, but the friars planned to hand over its ranches and vineyards to native Californians one day. If first impressions were reliable, all of this was to benefit one family, and its direction lay in the hands of one man: Don Iván de Montaraz.

Aurora suppressed a smile. That intimidating man appeared equal to the task of keeping an empire on course.

Back in Aurora's rooms the two made short work of settling in. "Thank you, María, for your informative tour and for helping me unpack."

"I will return to help you bathe and dress for dinner, Señorita." María disappeared around the doorframe into the hallway.

Aurora studied her quarters. A large mahogany bed beneath double windows dominated the room. Shutters slatted with twigs were folded back and late afternoon light flooded in. A smaller version of a kiva, the beehive fireplaces she'd seen downstairs, filled a corner. A wardrobe took up most of the wall near the fireplace and held her clothing.

"Well-appointed, he said. I'd call it luxurious."

If she stretched her legs, she'd still need a hop to reach the surface of that huge bed. If only Pía were here to share it. Aurora shoved the prayer bench from foot to bedside to provide a step. She hadn't seen two pillows on a bed since Mamá gave away Papá's at his death. The plank cots of the mission inhabitants had straw mattresses, one thin pillow, and a single blanket.

An arched opening led into the room Don Iván called her study. Through the closed door into Jocasta's room, she heard voices.

A small bookcase held several volumes. Books were costly and rare in her experience. There were treatises on plants and birds, helpful in planning lessons. And he had offered his extensive office library.

Whatever else I might need, he said. Who could possibly need more?

The thought should be comforting, but a sudden need for the familiar sent her back to her bedroom. She picked up her mother's prayer book, the one that first belonged to her grandmother, and stepped out onto the balcony. A shaded chair at one of the leather-topped tables beckoned. Colorful tendrils of scarlet bougainvillea and purple wisteria crept over the long railing from pots far below.

A breeze blew wisps of hair across Aurora's face. She adjusted combs to confine the offending tresses and opened her missal, but after a few minutes the sounds and smells of the garden, sharp and beguiling, lured her away.

Head tipped back, and eyes closed, she absorbed the fountain's enchanting gurgle. Out here Mamá seemed very near. She had enjoyed gardening and could create magic with a few stones and plants. She must have loved this place. Oh, if Aurora could reach out and touch her—see her lovely smile—hear her laugh once more. Sing with her.

Above the hum of insects, Aurora's voice rose in a musical prayer she and Mamá had created. An inquisitive dove settled on the balcony railing near her and added a soft, intermittent voice to hers.

A deep voice interrupted her peace and her song. Don Iván. He stood tall in the doorway to Jocasta's room, holding the hand of a little girl dressed in riding clothes.

"Nice song, Señorita. Not one I've heard." He signaled Aurora to continue. She finished the song and sang another before he led the child onto the balcony.

"She heard you and insisted upon meeting you. Señorita Rivera, may I present your student, Jocasta Juliana de Montaraz-Garza."

Lovely child. "Hello, Jocasta."

Jocasta offered a curtsy and stepped nearer. Wide-spaced black, black eyes shone in Jocasta's face. Unruly, reddish-brown hair sprang from her head, curling and thick, radiating health and vigor in the rosy light. Her sweet face showed her curiosity. She came up to the table and, placing her hands on either side of Aurora's face, drew it toward her.

"My eyes cannot see very far, so I have to bring things close. I still cannot see if you are pretty."

Aurora smiled at the solemn child. "My hair isn't nearly as beautiful as yours and my eyes are not as large as your dark ones. Mine are a greenish-brown."

"I have not learned the names of many colors," said Jocasta. "I do not need them since I cannot see much. I enjoy playing outdoors and riding horses with my father and uncles. They teach me everything I need to know."

Her Spanish was formal and the words clearly pronounced, with a faint challenge in their tone. Jocasta's command of words would have been impressive for a seven-year-old and the child was not yet five. Someone had developed her vocabulary.

"Do you like singing, Jocasta? I've been singing prayers to God. As I sat here gazing at your lovely garden, I decided to thank Him for plants and flowers He has created."

"I like songs about ranch life. Can you ride a horse? Can you rope a bull?"

"I can ride a horse, and I used to watch my father rope, but I've never tried to catch a bull. Perhaps we can ride together, but we'll leave the roping to your father and your uncles." Aurora looked at Don Iván in invitation.

Instead of joining the conversation, he reached down and lifted his daughter into his strong arms.

"*Niñita,* you will enjoy getting to know Señorita Rivera and have many good times together." He kissed Jocasta's cheek and said, "We must go in now. Luisa will soon come to help you dress for dinner. Until then, Señorita."

Aurora raised her eyebrows. Like father, like daughter. Two strong, intelligent minds. Challenge and opportunity. Life would not be boring.

She went inside to find María preparing a bath. What luxury to have hot water and a friendly assistant who wanted to help in any way she could.

María's kind face registered a smile. "Which dress shall I lay out?"

Aurora laughed. "Surprise me. Pick one of the three, whichever you like."

María beamed and chose the dark green one. "Beautiful with your glorious hair and your eyes," she said. "Your hair is streaked with the gold and brown of acorns."

If María had served at the same time as her Mamá, she must be in her early forties. Confidence marked her actions—a servant who knew her worth. A calm, gracious manner and gentle ministrations soothed away tensions. She was a treasure.

María insisted on fashioning Aurora's hair into an upswept style held by six small shell combs. "A style appropriate for dinners," she said. Obviously she wanted her mistress to make a good impression on the de Montaraz brothers. No guarantees there.

An hour later, Aurora descended the staircase with María. *Holy Father, I need more than a green dress and a new hairdo to gain the trust of four men concerning a little girl they love. Please help me be the woman You want me to be before them. To see them as You do, with concern for their souls. Please give me Your wisdom and love for Jocasta. Into Your hands.*

Iván paced his suite. He thought better on his feet. How would his brothers react to the new governess? Elías would be no problem, but Justo had been outspoken in his opposition from the start. Raúl was also against allowing her into the house, but he was forever a wild card with his eye for the ladies. And this one—

Iván sighed. He didn't need this complication,

but the die was cast. Father's wish took first place. Strange how he still felt bound to follow the man's dictates, even though they had caused great heart-ache in the past.

His brothers had also been willing to go along with Father's decrees until now. A vision of Aurora arose and his chest tightened. The woman was a game-changer. She unsettled a man. With her in the house, how long could he keep his brothers in line?

Four

Aurora paused in the doorway of the dining room. Four men rose to their feet, eyes riveted on her. Her gaze slid away. Faces could come later.

The *comedor* looked much grander than on her afternoon inspection, with its blaze of candles and a table set for service to immaculately-clad gentlemen.

Intriguing aromas filled the room. Dinner would not rely on the simple dishes of the mission, where friars and communicants shared meat the hunters brought or beef from the small herd of cattle. Her pupils took such pride in planting and caring for vegetables in the kitchen garden. A lump in her throat suddenly made swallowing difficult.

I must focus. She bowed her head for a moment, then straightened her spine to look into each face. "Good evening, *caballeros*. Jocasta." Her voice sounded huskier than usual.

The brothers stared at her with the same amazement she had noted earlier on Don Iván's face. What did they find so unusual about her? One by one, they turned toward their eldest brother.

"Good evening." From the head of the table, Don Iván came forward to escort her to her place on his left. Jocasta sat opposite her, solemn-faced, her head turning side to side as she squinted to discern details. How curious she must be to see how her new governess would be received.

No welcoming smiles. After all, they were aristocrats. The men wore the suits of gentlemen ranchers. No strong family resemblance among them. None of the others were as tall or as strongly built as Don Iván, although they were all well-muscled. They must be working ranchers and not the dandies some young Californios were.

"Señorita Rivera, my brothers. Just to Jocasta's right is Justo."

Aurora smiled at Jocasta and then nodded toward Justo, who bowed. Another handsome de Montaraz man. Black hair, as long as Don Iván's, was pulled back and tied at the base of Justo's well-shaped head. His face was long and tapered, but his mouth was generous and the lips full and curving, even without a smile. He made a swift appraisal, then his eyes narrowed, and he glared at Don Iván.

Her stance stiffened. Perhaps Justo's slight was the typical reaction of an aristocrat toward a servant at his table, but tension seemed to thicken the atmosphere. As if she'd walked into the midst of an argument. A young man at her side shifted his feet and she glanced toward him before turning to her host. Don Iván seemed to take no notice of Justo's accusatory stare. He continued the introductions.

"At the other end of the table is Raúl."

His hair and skin tone were lighter than either Don Iván or Justo's. A little taller than Justo, he was still several inches shorter than Don Iván, although his body reflected a comparably strong physique. Raúl's hair was cut much shorter than his brothers'. A rich, dark brown, its waves conformed to his head.

His eyes, brown and animated, were disquieting. They regarded her with an expression quite apart from Justo's hostility and the unreadable gaze of Don Iván. He studied her with an interest he did not try to hide. A little smile played at the corners of his mouth, and dimples showed as the smile widened. He assessed her face and body with evident pleasure.

Undressing me with his eyes! Aurora gasped at the disrespect. She turned to Don Iván. No help there. She was on her own.

Raúl bowed, but not low enough to break eye contact. "I'm more than pleased to make your acquaintance, Señorita."

His voice held an intimate tone, and he used familiar speech, employing the *tú*, rather than the more formal *usted.* Inappropriate on short acquaintance.

Of course, she was a servant, but she was also the daughter of an aristocratic mother and a respected father. She returned his heated gaze with what she hoped was chilling reproach.

The corners of Justo's mouth lifted in a cold smile. Don Iván leaned forward and frowned at Raúl and Justo, whose smiles faded.

Indicating the remaining brother at her side, Don Iván said, "Señorita Rivera, our youngest brother, Elías. He will reach his majority of eighteen years before many months, but long ago he became the best rancher among us with his understanding of animals."

Elías bowed. "*Bien venidos*. Welcome, Señorita Rivera."

Aurora liked his boyish face with its regular features and guileless gray eyes. His hair was no darker than Raúl's, but it was longer and he wore it unconfined like Don Iván. He raked a hand through it and waited for her to acknowledge him.

This she did with her first smile for one of the men. "Thank you, Don Elías."

There was an element of vulnerability about him. It made her want to know him better. Elías appeared pleased with the title she bestowed, and returned her smile with a big one of his own.

Justo huffed, a choked sound that reminded Aurora of a grumpy old hound Papá once had. He scowled at her and Elías and then at Don Iván, whose impenetrable gaze acknowledged nothing.

As they were seated, Justo and Raúl exchanged a glance that could only be described as contemptuous. They were less than delighted to have her among them and didn't mind showing their discontent. Surely they realized she was here only for Jocasta and had no interest in their business.

Don Iván said, "I told my brothers of your impressive qualifications, Señorita Rivera. We hope you will find life pleasant here at the ranch with Jocasta and her *caballeros*."

His words were ones she hoped to hear, but his manner did not match. His tone lacked warmth and he didn't look at her as he spoke. Instead he smiled at Jocasta, who had remained quiet throughout the introductions.

She squinted at Aurora and said, "*Tío* Justo says he can see no reason for an instructor when I have a father and three uncles who teach me. They understand life on a ranch and so must I."

Justo's arm reached behind Jocasta, and he glowered first at Aurora and then at his older brother. He meant to defend his niece and his position. Don Iván's face remained impassive and he didn't comment on Jocasta's speech.

So Justo was outspoken in his opposition to a tutor for his brother's child. Aurora refused to look in his direction. She smiled at Jocasta.

"Well, since we are both women, perhaps there are things we can learn from one another. With your father's permission, I will ask you to call me Señorita Aurora instead of *Maestra.* Teachers are often the best friends one can have. At least, my teachers at the mission were some of mine."

Jocasta looked doubtful, but said nothing. Aurora glanced at Justo, offering opportunity to explain his position. He turned away and made a comment to Raúl about tomorrow's work. Don Iván's gaze remained untroubled. He seemed in no hurry to establish a more gracious atmosphere.

So be it. The brothers' rejection would not depress her. She was here because God had called her for Jocasta.

A soothing sip from her water tumbler enabled her to appreciate intricate stenciling on the domed ceiling and the heavy carving of the fireplace mantel. Several times she sensed eyes upon her, but made no contact with anyone. Minutes passed in silence as servers finished bringing food into the room.

"Justo is our praying man, *Señorita,*" Don Iván said at last. "Justo, *por favor*."

Justo stood and offered a brief and formal blessing upon the food, and table attendants began serving from the sideboard. Jorge filled wine glasses and a smiling woman served delectable-looking plates.

There were quails braised in a smooth, dark sauce scented with cumin and other herbs, wild rice, several vegetables, and fresh, hot bread. Mixed fruits, rich and spicy, simmered in a chafing dish set over a small charcoal brazier at the end of a sideboard near Aurora.

Don Iván begin cutting up food on Jocasta's plate instead of leaving the task to a servant. He described each portion to Jocasta in an encouraging voice, just as Papá had done for her and Pía when they were small.

A sip of wine revealed a mellow vintage that hinted of fruit and flowers. She turned to Elías. "Fine wine. Your own?"

"True." He appeared pleased. "We make our own wines and brandy from a variety of grapes. I suppose you saw our vineyards?"

"Yes, Don Elías—stretching away apparently without end. Unmatched even by the vineyards of the Mission San Carlos." She smiled. "The food looks delicious. I have eaten quail only a few times."

From cutting up his daughter's food, Don Iván's black gaze caught hers. "I am afraid you cannot anticipate such food every night, Señorita. We are beef eaters in this house, with occasional dishes of lamb or pork. Our cook thought we should welcome you tonight with an offering more suited to a woman's taste." No smile softened his words.

Four sets of eyes watched her. Did the men believe she would demand a separate diet or try to influence theirs?

"I am used to very simple fare. The friars eat meagerly, not wanting to share in provisions unavailable to their converts, so food has never been of real importance to me."

Aurora forced herself to look into Don Iván's scrutiny. "My father was a *vaquero* and believed in the benefits of beef."

Next to her, Elías cleared his throat. Don Iván still watched. Color heated her cheeks. She needed to make her position clear.

"I do not expect you to make any adjustments. I am here at your request to become a special friend to Jocasta." She raised her chin.

Raúl barked a laugh. "*Caballeros,* among us has come an intelligent and spirited woman. She parries with a thrust of her sword, saying she's not interested in our business and serving notice upon us not to mix in hers." His brown gaze danced on her face.

"I brought no weapons into this house, Don Raúl. I wish only to put everyone at ease. I will give my best and report to Don Iván. I hope we can all be united by our interest in the well-being of Jocasta."

She looked from face to face as she spoke and smiled at the little girl. "Personally, Jocasta, I enjoy outdoor meals, and milk and fruit after lessons in the schoolroom."

Jocasta appeared pleased and even Justo showed a grudging respect. Don Raúl nodded in her direction, a wolfish smile on his face. The meal finished in civility if not camaraderie.

United in their outlook, Fray Peralta had warned. But why the mistrust? Even Don Iván appeared undecided, seeming ready to find her lacking. She had the feeling he did not truly want her in the house. So why had he asked her to come?

At the conclusion of the meal Luisa arrived for Jocasta. Aurora arose, ready to make her escape. Since her duties did not begin until the next day, she bid the brothers good evening, leaving them to enjoy the snifters of brandy and cigars waiting on a tray.

Instead of climbing the stairs to her quarters, she went out the front entry into the garden. It would be a good place to think.

Iván de Montaraz rose with his brothers and watched Aurora leave. After a moment he heard the front door close. He looked at each of his brothers in turn. Only Justo seemed ready to challenge him.

"Let's be seated," Iván said into the charged silence.

Jorge handed out cigars and filled their brandy glasses. Iván did not take a cigar and took only a sip of brandy before he stood.

"I will go to Jocasta," he said. "We'll speak tomorrow of your impressions of the young woman, hopefully not to rehash old arguments."

"Of course." Justo's voice sounded bitter. "Our thoughts can wait. The decision has been made by you alone, as is your custom."

Raúl muttered something under his breath and Elías looked uneasy.

"Enjoy your cigars, brothers." Iván left the dining

room, turned toward the front doors, and paused before he climbed the stairs. Give the new governess time with her thoughts.

Her appearance had been as big a shock for his brothers as it had for him—her beauty and spirit disturbing. Unarguably Father's daughter. He and his brothers had believed their future settled until Father's letter came to light.

Belated remorse, that letter, but typical of the man—deciding at the end to honor a moral claim on his name and fortune. No legal obligation involved, but it was Father's wish. The directive to bring her into the house jeopardized Iván's control over the others.

Already questioning my authority.

He shook his head and allowed a small smile to touch the corners of his lips. Aurora had managed to hold up well under her first trial by fire. Still, it was too early to tell if she was as worthy as Fray Peralta believed. Only time would tell. She had yet to deal with Jocasta.

Five

The nerve-shredding experience of the dining room behind her, Aurora let out a huge sigh and stepped into gathering darkness. The day had been a hot one, but with the setting sun, all of nature breathed in relief. The courtyard fountain trickled a sweet melody.

María had called the courtyard's center "frog square," a playful reference to the frog-filled Carmel River flowing nearby. Frog statuary adorned some of the pots surrounding the fountain, and at its center, water spouted upward from a frog-like stone creature's mouth. Jocasta probably enjoyed playing here.

Aurora strolled down the long driveway to the arched entry, now secured by wrought-iron gates. A spoonful of stars was visible in the fading light. In the hills a faraway campfire glowed. Probably that of Basque shepherds guarding one of the ranch flocks.

Papá would know. *Oh, Papá, the world is not the same without you.* No one on this ranch cared about her. Was she now to drift through her days, bumping up against others but never really connecting?

She rubbed her arms. Enough. Her situation did offer new possibilities. Perhaps she'd find answers to long-held questions.

Grandpapá Rivera had come from Mexico City with the father of Don Iván. Papá had been born on this ranch. After years of work, Don León had named him *caporal,* second-in-command. Papá told stories of wrangling cattle and fighting fires. But he had never mentioned Don León, although he must have enjoyed the owner's trust.

Why had he left to care for smaller mission herds? And Mamá—where were her stories of Señora de Montaraz or the brothers? Don Iván and Raúl would have been children when she worked here, but she'd never mentioned them.

So many questions.

The brothers' resistance baffled her. Perhaps they feared Jocasta would become too fond of the new teacher to give them her usual attention. *I must guard against any intrusion into the family's structure.*

"Stop it! I came out to enjoy the garden." She didn't have to understand those men to fulfill her calling. Leave them in God's hands.

Aurora turned back and chose a pathway that meandered between fragrant plantings toward a wall on the west. Through an arched gate smothered in passion flowers lay a more formal garden with a reflecting pool.

Beyond the pool's perimeter, the path led to a large cypress. The garden's layout had to be a woman's plan. Too many delicate touches, romantic statuary, and vignettes. The mother of those puzzling men had created a sanctuary—and Mamá may have helped her. The thought was almost like a hug.

"A grandmother would approve of a swing for her granddaughter," Aurora whispered. "Mamá insisted on one for Pía and me, and we spent many happy hours there. I'll speak to Don Iván."

Above her the great cypress murmured, telling its secrets to the night. A wrought-iron bench near the reflecting pool beckoned. A perfect spot to sit for a time and pray.

Perhaps three quarters of an hour passed in pleasant reverie before the crunch of footsteps on the gravel path broke her thoughts. She turned to watch Don Iván's lithe approach. Her stomach performed an odd little flip.

"We knocked at your door. Jocasta wished to tell you good night. She is with Luisa now." He stood over her, outlined in moonlight.

Aurora squinted up at him. "I did not mean to disappoint Jocasta, Don Iván. You said my duties would not begin until tomorrow, so I decided to explore your lovely gardens before I retired."

"I meant no reproach, Señorita Rivera. I was concerned that you might be alone somewhere regretting your decision to come. Try to be patient with all of us, and I believe things will work out."

Really? He'd been less than helpful at dinner.

"Please sit with me if you have a moment." The words were out before she had time to rethink them.

He sat, crossed his long legs, and turned her way. "Señorita?"

She felt the sting of a frown she couldn't see and chose her words. "Señor de Montaraz, I intend to offer my best."

His stillness was complete. He was listening.

"I will try to be a positive influence in Jocasta's life. I believe we will eventually become close, although it may take some time to win her confidence."

Still no response. If only she could see his expression. "I ask you to trust my intentions and my methods. It will make progress much easier."

Aurora thought his eyes narrowed in the shadowed face. She waited through a silence.

"I will try, Señorita Rivera. I promise nothing, but I will try. I am not by nature a trusting man." His deep voice was gentle. Warmer than she'd expected.

He stood. For an instant she felt bereft, not wanting him to leave. He hesitated, staring down at her. Had her stray thought showed on her face?

"Good night." He took two steps and turned back. "If I can believe in anyone upon such short acquaintance, somehow I think it is you, Señorita."

A big *if.* She watched his departing figure and sighed. Iván de Montaraz stirred something inside her. Something she shouldn't encourage.

Farther into the garden, deep in reflection, her steps slowed. The thought of returning to the house held no appeal.

"Pray large, Fray Peralta says. I must not be afraid to ask God for big things." Aurora spoke the words aloud. Hearing truth helped cement it in her mind.

The de Montaraz men were large; their house and ranch huge. She was one small woman in unfamiliar surroundings. How could God possibly use her among these strong men? She began to pray for the seemingly impossible.

Minutes passed. Moonlight trickled through trees and dappled the pathway. With a freshening breeze the night cooled and she walked faster, arms hugging her body. A turn and then another. Which shadowy path led back to the main one?

In the dense shade of a corner protected by a pomegranate shrub, she bumped into a man. His arms came out to steady her.

"Don Iván, I suppose I became confused, but you need not have returned. I think I am on the right path now."

"The right path, Señorita, but the wrong don." It was the voice of Raúl. "I wondered where you went after Iván returned without you. It seems he left it to me to get you back inside, but there is little reason to hurry, *¿verdad*? Stroll with me. I have questions for you."

Oh, no. Aurora stepped back and said, "I am ready to return to the house. The evening is suddenly much cooler."

He stripped off his short leather jacket and wrapped it around her shoulders. "I have questions, Señorita Rivera, but I do not want you to be uncomfortable. Never uncomfortable in my presence."

His Spanish was formal and his words respectful, but she remembered his overly-welcoming eyes and the glances he exchanged with Don Justo. He'd deliberately tried to unsettle her.

His voice became low and persuasive. "We will go back slowly as I think how to word my inquiries." He steered Aurora along, close beside him.

It was a greater familiarity than she could allow. A gentleman did not initiate physical contact with a lady, let alone hold her near him in a controlling grip.

She stopped and removed his hand. "May I speak frankly, Don Raúl? I have questions of my own, so perhaps this is a fortuitous meeting."

"Of course. Any meeting in moonlight is desirable." His voice held the whisper of silk.

Aurora quickened her steps. "Do you have doubts about my suitability as tutor for your niece? I sensed hesitancy in all of you tonight."

When he didn't respond, she added, "I did not seek the position. Friar Peralta persuaded me to come at Don Iván's request. If my presence is unwelcome, I should know why." She stopped and faced him.

He studied her, apparently deep in thought. A finger rubbed along his lower lip.

"I hope we can deal in honesty, Don Raúl. If you have reservations, please express them. I need cooperation from the family if Jocasta is to progress as she should."

"Very well. I shall be quite frank so that we can get off on a proper footing. My questions are grave ones, and you may not wish to deal with them, but I hope you will, as they must be answered."

Had she misjudged him?

He pulled her into his arms. She froze, staring up at the smile playing at the corners of his mouth.

"Do you know how beguiling you are, wrapped in this soft blanket of light? Can we meet here each night to dance in the moonbeams?"

Aurora struggled, but he held her.

"Don't take offense, little teacher. Our primary purpose will be to check on my niece's progress. If we tire of talk, I can bring my guitar. Or there are other possibilities." He tugged her closer.

Aurora broke his grip, managing to strip the jacket from her shoulders and push it toward him before she stalked away.

"Must you love me and leave me in this fashion?" His laughter echoed as she strode toward the house.

After leaving Aurora, Iván neared the staircase to his balcony. A cigar glowed in the shadows of Raúl's patio. Raúl would go after the girl.

Iván took a seat and waited. He watched Raúl search for Aurora and their encounter beside the pomegranate. Should he interfere? She would have to deal with Raúl at some point. He couldn't hear their words, but he wasn't surprised to see her successfully struggle to escape his embrace.

She had spirit. She also had an openness about her faith he'd never encountered. Comfortable with the idea of a God who led her. How could she think it was God who brought her to the ranch? Don León de Montaraz brought her—against the better judgment of all his sons.

The friar had assured him she knew nothing of Father's letter and nothing of her true parentage. Her willingness to come could not be a ploy to claim an inheritance. She wasn't capable of duplicity.

Where did that notion come from? All women were devious if it served their purposes. He should know.

Had he made a mistake in asking her to come? A part of him regretted exposing an innocent girl to Justo's self-righteous scorn and Raúl's womanizing. Too late now.

Perhaps it was better. She might leave on her own before any damage was done and his duty would be discharged. Pain and disillusionment were inevitable if she stayed.

He sighed. The sins of fathers were well and truly visited upon their sons. And their daughters.

Six

Jocasta. Their first day. Aurora prayed as she dressed. She waited in Jocasta's room for Luisa to wake her. Leave the familiar routine in place. There'd be changes enough. The little girl rose and washed without murmur.

"I'll bring your dress, Jocasta." Aurora chose a serviceable robin's-egg blue one from the many crowded into the armoire.

"Not that one. I want my pink dress with big pockets. Luisa will get it."

Pink Valencian brocade. Totally unsuitable for a schoolroom where it might be stained with chalk or paint.

"Jocasta..." Aurora paused. Better to choose her battles. "You're an early riser. I woke in time to watch the sun peek over the hills."

No answer.

"May I brush your hair? I brought you two little combs my father carved for me."

Jocasta shrugged. "If I could see well enough I

would style my own hair. I am not a baby."

Aurora brushed the ends of her unruly hair to remove tangles; then worked higher until the mass was orderly. "Now the combs." From a center part, Aurora placed a comb in each side, replicating her own hairdo. She handed Jocasta a mirror.

"I feel the combs, but I cannot see them." Jocasta removed one and peered at it. "How did your father make them?"

"He carved them from shells we gathered on the beach. The combs are made from the shells' insides. A material called mother-of-pearl. It's iridescent, meaning it reflects many colors. I'm wearing two like them, only a bit larger." Aurora replaced the comb.

Jocasta pulled both combs from her hair. "They hurt my head. I will wear one of my ribbons. Pick one for me the same color as my dress and give it to Luisa."

A bit of rebellion, but expected. Don Iván had warned her. Aurora chose a rose-colored ribbon. "I'll keep the combs for you." She knelt eye-to-eye with Jocasta. "When you have a request of me or of Luisa, you must say 'please.' I do the same. So does your father. It is polite and a part of being grown up."

Jocasta's brows drew together. She didn't answer and sidled toward the doorway. Aurora reached for her hand to lead her down the stairs, but the little girl pulled away and rushed forward.

Luisa gasped. "She is not allowed alone on the stairs!"

Feeling along the railing, Jocasta hurried down the stairs, and stumbled on the third step. Aurora lunged for Jocasta's arm and caught it.

"You were going too fast. There are many steps

on the stairs. Each is made of stone and will leave a bruise if you fall. Please take my hand. You can count the steps as we go." Surprisingly, Jocasta stayed with her as they counted aloud.

"Twenty-four bumps and bruises," Jocasta said. She frowned.

"You know a great deal about numbers. Yes, that many bumps and bruises might mean days in bed or even a broken bone. Broken bones hurt. I know, because I broke my arm when I was just a little older than you."

"On the stairs?"

"No. I was thrown from a horse as my father taught me to ride." Aurora looked around and said, "Can you guide me? I'm ready for breakfast."

"This way." Across the foyer and its morning's dance of rainbows, Jocasta headed down a short hallway, Aurora in tow.

Four men stood in the same order as the evening before. They welcomed Jocasta and scrutinized her tutor. Aurora looked down and sighed.

Holy Father, please give me Your patience and wisdom among these hostile men. Do not let me bend before them if it is Your will that I remain.

Don Iván held her chair and bid Aurora good morning, then seated his daughter and himself and asked a brief question about the day's studies. His attention was on his daughter.

Aurora's answer was as short as his inquiry and he turned to study her for a moment. She raised her chin and sent him a starchy look.

A tiny smile lifted one corner of his mouth before he turned away and began cutting up Jocasta's omelet of eggs, sausage, and a few garden vegetables.

"Your toasted bread is at the top of your plate, little one, and your juice on the right as always."

Her resentment melted. He was so caring with his daughter. Like Papá.

Iván looked from Aurora to Jocasta and allowed a smile. "A big day. Your first day of school." Jocasta shrugged.

From the other end of the table Raúl spoke up. "Any chore you need done in the schoolroom, Señorita? I'm not certain you know, but a man can be most useful."

A mocking smile teased his lips. She didn't answer her handsome tormentor, but Don Iván raised his eyes to Raúl. There it was again—that intent, absorbing gaze.

Leaving his breakfast unfinished, Raúl stood, staring at his older brother.

Don Iván chewed thoughtfully at a bite. "Have you completed the inventory of hides I asked of you yesterday?" His voice held no special urgency.

Raúl flushed and his eyes flashed. "I will have it in your hands before noon," he snapped, tossing his napkin down as he left the table.

Oho! All is not unity between the brothers.

Justo turned his dark, accusing stare on Aurora and threw down his napkin. He rose to follow, Elías on his heels with a hasty excuse.

Fascinating, the way Iván controlled his brothers. His word was law. But surely he wouldn't expect unquestioning obedience from her. She needed freedom to express her own ideas in guiding Jocasta.

Don Iván looked unruffled by the hurried departures. He lifted Jocasta's small glass. "Finish it, sweet one."

Jocasta took two sips. "Take me with you, Papá, to saddle Diego."

"All of it." He watched until Jocasta drained the glass and turned to Aurora.

"This morning is as good a time as any for you to pick a mount, Señorita. I am sure Jocasta will wheedle rides. Of course, the two of you must never ride unaccompanied."

"I trust your judgment as to a mount, Don Iván. You know your horses."

"Corazón, Papá—Corazón. Please," begged Jocasta. She turned to Aurora. "My favorite. She is called Corazón, *Maestra,* because she has a heart-shaped blaze on her face."

"Your teacher asked you to address her as Señorita Aurora."

"*Perdóname,* Señorita Aurora."

"Of course, Jocasta. I'm eager to see Corazón."

At the stables Don Iván brought out a lovely black mare and an ornately-decorated side saddle. Aurora stood back with Jocasta as he saddled Corazón.

"I believe you will have no problem trusting me with your daughter on a horse. I have been riding alone since I was younger than Jocasta, but I understand your need to see for yourself."

Don Iván's gaze lifted to hers and one brow raised. Aurora colored. She hadn't meant her observation to insinuate at his controlling nature.

"A beautiful saddle. Your mother's?" At his nod she said, "My mother loved to ride."

"Mine did not. Father tried to encourage her, saying it would improve her health, but she resisted."

Aurora stepped nearer and he swung her into the

saddle as if she were a feather. For a moment their faces were level. His scent filled her nostrils—sandalwood soap and fresh linen. His warm breath was on her cheek.

She grabbed at the saddle horn and pulled herself into place, blessing her foresight in wearing pantalets. "Coming up here with me, Jocasta?"

Clear relief flashed across Don Iván's face when Jocasta chose to ride with him.

Jocasta said, "Are the blackbirds here, Papá?"

"Yes. They're settled in the corral, squabbling as usual over the bits of grain left by the donkeys and horses." He motioned for Aurora to go ahead of him. "Proceed, Señorita."

He wanted to assess her riding ability. She felt his watchful gaze as she guided the mare toward the gate held open by a stable boy.

What he saw must have reassured him. Don Iván took the lead, putting his mount into a lope as they headed toward the river.

Ahead two *vaqueros* wrestled with a young bull. Other cattle grazed nearby, unconcerned for the predicament of their fellow herd member.

Past weedless vineyards the three rode through a land of beef and wine, much like that surrounding the mission. Soothing, after hours spent in the unaccustomed opulence of the house and the unsettling company of its men. Here were country people engaged in her father's work.

Jocasta rode slumped against Don Iván's chest, her face upturned to the sun. A pity she couldn't see the landscape.

They reached the orchard and she said, "Stop, Papá. I like the smells."

"Describe them precisely, daughter."

"Damp earth, wood, and other plants. Ferns?"

"Exactly. Like the ones growing in the conservatory. You're very observant. Listen closely. You can hear the ring of a red-headed woodpecker's beak as he taps out his rhythm on a dead tree trunk not far away."

Aurora wanted to clap. *Good for you, Papá.* Very much the educator for his daughter. If he became her ally, the little girl could enter new worlds.

Jocasta's face glowed with pride. "Corazón likes apples, Señorita Aurora. I will pick one for her and you will see how much she enjoys them." She squinted at the trees.

Don Iván described several of the fruits to her. "Yes, that one," she said of the third apple. He lifted her from the saddle until she had the fruit in her hands. "Now one for me."

"I think, *mí tesoro,* the apples need longer to ripen before you'll enjoy one, but they should be just right for Corazón and Diego. We'll get one for him, too, and one for good measure."

She was his treasure. The controlling Don Iván had a gentle, perceptive side. What was his story? And how had Jocasta's mother died at such a young age?

Fray Peralta must know more of the men than he could tell her, bound as he was by his vows. María might offer information about the past of the intriguing de Montaraz men—enigmatic Don Iván, flirtatious Raúl, antagonistic Justo, and sweet Elías. She would have known them as children.

Their mistrust was irrational; almost as if she had the power to change their lives. Ridiculous. She was one of their many servants.

"I'm ready to ride on Corazón, Papá."

Iván lifted Jocasta to Aurora's waiting arms. For a moment she thought he'd offer advice, but he turned Diego toward home.

Jocasta clutched the apples close to her body. "I chose well. You will see."

Enchanting, the feel of the child in her arms and the jasmine fragrance of her hair. All too soon the three entered the stable yard and Iván's strong arms plucked teacher and pupil from the saddle as one.

He split the fruit with the knife from his sash, so that even the pet fawn of the stable yard enjoyed a portion from Jocasta's hand.

"I picked the best apples, Señorita Aurora. The animals are all happy."

"I'm sure they're grateful." Her cheeks heated under the unexpected warmth of Don Iván's glance.

"Work hard today, my daughter. Learn something new from your teacher. You can tell me tonight." He touched his hat, mounted, and rode away. Aurora watched until he reached the crest of a hill. Don Iván stood in the stirrups, and waved his hat.

"Your father saluted, Jocasta. He expects great things of us. Let's begin our adventure in the school room so you can surprise him tonight with your good work." Aurora took the young girl's hand and led her to the big house.

Seven

If only the rest of the day had gone as well as the orchard adventure. Jocasta roamed around the schoolroom while Aurora read to her.

"Do you have a favorite doll, Jocasta? Let's bring her to enjoy the story with us."

Esperanza joined them. She bounced up and down as the story finished. She danced on the table while Jocasta sang only a few words of a new song. The reluctant pupil wandered away from the study table.

"I'm hungry. Tell Luisa to bring lunch." She stared at Aurora. "Please," she added. Jocasta headed for the doorway onto the balcony, Esperanza trailing behind on the floor. "Can we eat outside, Señorita Aurora?"

"Good idea. I'll ring for Luisa. While we wait you can help me set out the art supplies. After lunch we will make a tree of real twigs and leaves. Our schoolroom needs some art on the walls."

Jocasta picked at her lunch, even a fruit salad of plums and peaches, but made short work of the flan pudding and two cookies. Aurora finished her seafood stew and began spooning up her pudding.

Jocasta's mouth turned down. "I want to share your pudding. Mine is gone."

"Mine would be, too, if I hadn't taken time to finish my other food. Sweets are eaten at the end of a meal, after the more healthful food Luisa brings." Aurora smiled and offered Jocasta a small cookie, but no pudding.

The art lesson was mediocre at best. Jocasta smeared glue on a wooden plank with gusto, but her interest soon flagged. The twig tree had few leaves. Most of them went into Esperanza's apron pocket.

Aurora suggested a trip to the garden to cut a bouquet for the dinner table.

"I have never seen flowers on the dinner table. Will my *caballeros* like them?"

"Gentlemen enjoy bouquets."

Jocasta skipped into the garden. "Good smells, Señorita Aurora."

"We can choose several kinds of flowers and learn their names. We must be careful of thorns on the roses. I'll cut them and put them in our basket, but you can pick others."

The only suitable container for the results of Jocasta's enthusiastic harvest was one of the large Talavera vases atop the china cabinet. Aurora brought it to the schoolroom work table and handed Jocasta the magnifying glass Don Iván had provided.

"See how the vase design repeats some of the flowers' colors?"

Jocasta repeated names and colors as they placed the blooms. "I think we need more flowers."

"The vase won't hold more. We can create a new arrangement when this one wilts. I think it will look lovely on the dining table."

Luisa carried the heavy vase and Aurora held Jocasta's hand down the stairs. Before Luisa placed the arrangement, Jocasta buried her nose in a rose.

"This red rose smells good." She cut a glance Aurora's way. "Red rose. Golden yarrow, orange poppies, and white daisies."

"Right you are on all counts." Aurora pointed out several others. "Perhaps we can move our easels outside and paint in the garden tomorrow."

Jocasta brightened; then hid her smile. "Perhaps."

Aurora smothered a laugh. Her father's daughter.

The aroma of flowers greeted teacher and pupil as they entered the *comedor* that evening. None of the men commented on the arrangement. Jocasta seemed to take her cue from them and sat without mentioning the afternoon's achievement.

After Justo's blessing, Don Iván turned to Jocasta. "What did you learn today, daughter?"

"*Nada*—nothing important. We did pick all these flowers. I learned some of their names and colors and helped arrange them for the table."

Don Iván turned to Aurora with a raised eyebrow.

Aurora met his gaze and nodded. "That was the sole subject Jocasta turned her efforts toward today. She found no interest in stories, artwork, or music, but she enjoyed the garden. Perhaps tomorrow she will be ready for new experiences."

Don Justo's gaze flickered with heat. "She is like the de Montaraz men, Señorita. We prefer to follow our own interests."

"Perhaps that is true," Aurora said with a little nod and turned her attention to her food. Don Raúl barked a laugh from his end of the table, but she didn't look his way.

Don Iván's words were firm. "New experiences can be good, Jocasta. The flowers are lovely and expertly arranged, but that should not have been your only effort today. Tomorrow I expect you to share a lesson you learned indoors."

Jocasta looked to Aurora and so did the brothers. Aurora said nothing, careful not to allow her expression to change. The little girl continued her meal in silence.

Don Justo huffed his grumpy sound and shook his head, still staring at Aurora. After a moment, Don Raúl complimented the arrangement. Jocasta smiled.

"It took a long time to gather the flowers, *Tío*, and to arrange them. We worked hard."

"It has been a while since our table was graced by flowers," Don Iván said with a smile. "You ladies added much enjoyment to the meal." Jocasta beamed, the relationship between father and daughter restored.

At meal's end, Aurora accompanied Luisa and Jocasta to the stairs. "I'm going into the garden tonight. Did you know some flowers go to sleep, Jocasta? I'll say goodnight to them." She had in mind a morning glory vine and purple wine cups she'd seen earlier. "And the moonflower plant we saw this afternoon wakes only at night. I'll say hello to it."

"May I go with you? Please? I have never seen a sleepy flower."

Aurora knelt in front of her. "I'm proud of you for saying 'please.' It shows you appreciate what others do for you. We always say please and thank you to people, just as we thank God for what He does for us."

Hand in hand the two went out the front entry. Aurora glimpsed Don Iván standing in the entrance of the dining room, cigar in hand.

Raúl tried to brush past his brother in the doorway, but Iván caught his arm. "Do not follow the ladies into the garden tonight, *hermano*."

Raúl felt himself flush. "Thank you, big brother, for your very welcome advice."

He sat on his terrace, watching Aurora and Jocasta, but he didn't enter the garden. "Iván must have seen us from his balcony last night," he muttered. "That spirited one wouldn't have asked for his help—but she may in time." He chuckled, flicking ash from his cigar.

The next evening Aurora and Jocasta stood at the upper railing when the men came in. Iván called up to Jocasta, "Come down, you two. We have a surprise. Señorita Aurora suggested it."

A swing hung in the shade of a large hardwood tree. Don Iván explained it to Jocasta as she was reaching for a rope. She bounced into the seat. "Hold onto the ropes tightly, *niña.*"

He placed his strong hands over hers and pushed, following the swing with an anxious gaze. The uncles all stood near and Aurora held her breath.

Within minutes, Jocasta flew through the air, with cries of "Higher! Higher!"

Raúl enticed her off a half hour later with his guitar. He began a song of the range and Aurora joined in on the second chorus. Even Don Iván added his deep voice when Jocasta pleaded. Aurora's heart warmed to be one of the family and not the outsider.

She used afternoon swing sessions as privileges earned for Jocasta's sporadic attempts at cooperation in schoolroom lessons. She watched for the moments when Jocasta displayed interest in a subject and planned similar lessons.

Jocasta's concentration went beyond the ability of most four-year-olds in those moments. And her extensive vocabulary was unusual. *What a privilege to guide this quick mind.*

Aurora worked around Jocasta's insistence on frequent changes of pace. She'd been used to ordering Luisa about the house and gardens. A gentle bridling of that desire to control was in order. Two Don Iván's in the house were too many.

Jocasta declared on the tenth morning, "I do not like school. I am going to ask Father to send you away. Why should I try to learn the songs you teach? Only the songs of *Tío* Elías and *Tío* Raúl belong on this ranch. They are about cattle and horses and life on the range."

Aurora nodded. "I'm learning them. One can never know too many songs. As for sending me away, it was your father's idea that I come. He believes you'll enjoy learning new things."

Jocasta's face turned mulish.

"There's a huge world outside this ranch stretching away even across oceans, Jocasta. God has filled it with wondrous things. In fact, as I prayed this morning, an idea came to me: a trip to the beach to explore and to study."

A faint gleam of interest appeared in two black

eyes. "Study beside the ocean?"

"Yes. Perhaps on a day when *Tío* Elías is not too busy he can accompany us. We'll see how many different seashells we find. We'll wash them in the sea and bring back a sack of sand to make a nature display for our schoolroom. We can even learn names of the little animals that made the shells. Your father has many books to help us. Learning is fun, Jocasta."

Excitement built in teacher and pupil as they planned their trip, formulating questions to answer by observations at the shore. Aurora spoke of tides and winds, the possibility of seeing a ship arrive in port, and of how sailors used the ocean to go wherever they wished. She mentioned distant lands and people, and showed Jocasta objects in the house that came from across the sea. The discussion veered into the use of maps and even into finding one's way navigating by stars.

"Your idea of looking for birds is a good one, Jocasta. Perhaps we can find descriptions of them in your father's books. We can take our paints and create a beach scene. We'll decorate our schoolroom with pictures of what we learn. The surf's music may inspire us to create a song."

"Maybe," said Jocasta. "Can we plan a picnic?"

"Definitely. Some foods travel better than others. Sofía and Luisa can help us with that."

When they heard Don Iván's voice in the foyer, Jocasta rushed to the railing, her hand in Aurora's. "When can we go to the shore? We will study by the sea. Collect shells and look for birds—"

"Whoa, *hija*. *Mas despacio*. I can't keep up with you." Don Iván climbed the stairs. His amused eyes met Aurora's and he grinned, looking so boyish that she laughed. Jocasta chattered on about all they could learn at the seashore, which foods would travel well, and what they would wear to swim in the waves. Aurora found herself adding details and requests.

Don Iván laughed. "I think Elías can be spared for a day. I may go along, as well. You two make the day seem like one not to be missed. I can check at the port for my latest shipment. It will have to be one day next week, however, since we are planning roundups on two ranges this week."

A good idea to have a few days before their outing. Aurora wanted to make a bathing costume for herself and one for Jocasta. She also needed to do some research on shore birds and blessed the extensive library in Don Iván's *oficina*.

At dinner, Jocasta babbled from the doorway to her chair. Don Raúl at once asked to be included on the trip, but Don Iván said he'd be needed to oversee things. "You can go on the next outing."

Raúl turned a wicked smile Aurora's way. "I'll begin plans at once. One cannot be too prepared for such a possibility."

Aurora ducked her head to keep from returning the smile. Don Raúl never missed an opportunity to flirt. Outrageous man, but witty. She would, however, ask María or Luisa to accompany them on any trip with *Tío* Raúl.

With María's help, in two days Aurora completed her bathing costume. It was a shift sewed from lightweight canvas. Worn over pantalets, the tunic was weighted at the hem to prevent it floating up. It would fill with water and conceal her womanly figure.

She showed it to Don Iván.

He shook his head. "You will not be able swim in that cumbersome suit. Please, Señorita, do not burden my daughter with a similar one."

A man did not understand the need for modesty, but the one she and María made for Jocasta was made of lightweight cotton and shorter.

Perhaps the beach adventure would open her sweet pupil to the joys of learning about God and His creation. Maybe even Don Iván could better understand the teaching methods Mamá had passed on. Two large goals for just one day, but God could make anything possible. Pray large.

Eight

Aurora sighed. Exasperating morning. Jocasta's worst yet, even allowing for the fact that she was tired from too much sun and sea.

The thought of yesterday's beach adventure brought a smile. The only blot had been the unwieldy swimming costume. Don Iván's prediction that she'd be unable to swim in it proved annoyingly true.

Jocasta had been in her element, instructing her father and *Tío* Elías what to do. She'd supervised the placement of her easel and pail of tools and rattled off questions to be answered by "observation." The word cost Don Iván a rare smile cast in Aurora's direction.

"You will have to be my eyes," Jocasta insisted. "Be precise."

Don Iván had used *precise* in the orchard and Jocasta remembered, just as she recalled Aurora's use of *observation* in the classroom. Amazing memory.

Together they had built a sandcastle. Jocasta giggled as she watched the waves swallow it. A frolic in the ocean brought more laughter. Aurora was pleased with the little girl's efforts in painting an abstract scene. While collecting seashells with her father, Jocasta kicked sand into Don Iván's hair, and earned a thorough dunking.

Laughter, good food, a horseback ride through the waves, and some serious study. Perhaps Don Iván learned that Aurora was an intentional instructor with a well-thought-out teaching plan, even if the teacher could not design appropriate beach wear.

But the good feeling didn't carry over into this morning's classroom. Aurora finally removed swing privileges for the afternoon. Jocasta stormed downstairs, her hand in Luisa's, filled with indignation and hurt feelings. Don Iván sent word he would see Aurora in his office at one o'clock.

She touched the crucifix at her neck before she knocked on the door. It opened to reveal Don Iván's implacable face—his expression as remote and set as the face on a coin.

"Come in, Señorita." He strode to his desk and indicated a chair. "Please be seated."

Aurora's toes didn't touch the floor in the big chair until she squirmed forward. She sat up ramrod straight and went to the heart of the matter. "Jocasta goes over my head, and makes discipline a matter only for you, Don Iván. I need your trust in gaining her cooperation."

A muscle rippled along its jaw, but the coin face did not speak. Iván de Montaraz encouraged awkward silences and the pressure that came with them. She met his intimidating stare.

"I rely on motivation, rather than imposing my will on Jocasta. When I withhold a privilege, it is because it has not been earned."

A long finger began tapping the desk. After eight taps, Aurora said, perhaps more firmly than she intended, "I can open doors for Jocasta, but she must enter. Her attitude holds her back."

How tiresomely pedantic. If she was to earn his confidence she must make him see how much she cared for Jocasta. The little girl had stolen her heart.

The coin's mouth at last spoke. "Jocasta can be difficult. I will take her for the afternoon and give you time away. But try to more understanding. First an accident impaired her sight. Then she lost her mother. Jocasta has only me to count on in that dark world of hers."

"The very heart of the matter, Don Iván. Please help her see that she can rely on me, as well. I care so much about her." Her voice shook.

Wrong, wrong, wrong. Iván would have no use for an emotional woman. Iván? She meant Don Iván. She could think of the other brothers without titles, but not Don Iván.

She rose. "I will be present at dinner."

The promise of the afternoon banished any disappointment. She, of all people, could sympathize with Jocasta's love of the outdoors. Don Iván's emphasis on the discipline of a classroom wasn't right for Jocasta at this point. The idea of moving even more studies outdoors deserved thought.

As Aurora walked away from the house, *vaqueros* ahead of her drove horses over a hill. Birds called with trills and whistles from nesting spots near the river.

Topping a rise she heard the water's murmur.

Around another bend the river beckoned, sparkling like diamonds as it tumbled and uncoiled its way out of the high country. Swirls and eddies rippled and rolled their way toward the not-too-distant sea.

A clearing at the water's edge held a sycamore dipping its lanky branches into the water. She sat on a rock in its dappled shade and leaned back, taking slow and easy breaths.

A red-legged frog leaped from concealment to capture a hovering insect. Farther out a green heron stood motionless, one leg drawn up, ready to spear his prey.

"Take care, red-legged frog, or you may become lunch." Aurora sighed. "I've missed the river."

The Carmel River was a paradise of trout, sun perch, eels, frogs, and crabs. As a girl living among children of the mission, she'd spent hours wading, fishing, and swimming. Oh, for the freedom and security of those bygone days!

Before he became too ill, Papá had accompanied Pía and her on outings. They fished or picnicked and shared stories of their childish adventures. Papá had laughed and talked of his experiences on the range.

Surrendering to the water's lure, Aurora removed her shoes and stockings. Upstream she spotted what might be a cove overhung with willows. Bunching her skirts to form a pocket for shoes and stockings, she waded toward it. Her toes chilled and paled in the shallow water. She picked her way past a boulder guarding the view.

"How lovely!" Protected by its screen of willows, the cove was hers alone, a secluded sanctuary. The tang of the sea mixed with cool river smells and the perfume of flowers and grass. Swallows darted about, twinkling like black stars against a blue sky.

"With Jocasta's quick mind, opportunities are limitless. I need her trust and that of her father and uncles." Elías offered shy friendship. Raúl was civil if Don Iván was present, but his eyes and suggestive smiles showed his real feelings. She preferred the honest hostility of Justo.

No one in sight and only the sounds of nature. Aurora slipped out of her new dress and petticoat. She waded out into sun-warmed shallows until the water reached her shoulders. By then she was in the middle of the inlet. A good place to bring Jocasta. The water was sweet and pure.

Aurora paddled lazily outward into the river proper. Breaking into her strong stroke, she pitted herself against the current. After several minutes of the cold, swift flow, she was ready to return to shore—but the cove had an unwelcome visitor.

Raúl maneuvered his horse near the shrub where she had hung her dress and petticoat. On instinct, Aurora turned back into the river. Over her shoulder, she saw him goad his wild-eyed stallion after her.

"*¡Hola!* A little mermaid."

She faced him, treading water. "If you come any nearer on that animal, I may drown beneath his legs."

"You're right, sweet one." Raúl tossed first one boot then the other with his jacket onto the shore. He hung his hat on the saddle horn, and slid into the river.

His well-trained stallion left the water, shook himself, and began grazing about. By some minor miracle, the hat still hung from the saddle.

Aurora struck a diagonal course toward the bank, swimming as fast as she could, but Raúl's powerful strokes carried him there well ahead of her. He crawled up onto the bank and stooped, arms and hands outstretched.

Though conscious of her wet and clinging clothing, she let him pull her up. If she stayed in the water, he would only come in after her. He didn't stop until she was in his arms.

"Mmmm. A pleasant surprise to find the very proper teacher sporting in her underclothes." His breath was warm in her ear and his afternoon beard rasped at her cheek.

"Thank you for your assistance, Don Raúl." Her arms and shoulders tensed as Aurora tried to step away, but he held her. She glared at him. "Please let me get to my clothes. I am cold."

"I can warm you." His smile broadened and he pulled her closer.

"Don Raúl, take your hands off me."

His arms tightened. She pushed back with all her strength and raised her hand to deliver a stinging slap, but he caught it.

"'Teach not thy lips such scorn: for they were made for kissing, lady, not for such contempt.' The Englishman could have written those words for you, Aurora."

Had he quoted Shakespeare? She stood her ground, what little she had in his strong arms, and frowned.

"Don Raúl, I am a paid servant in your house, but I am also the charge of Friar Elizondo Peralta and under the protection of your brother. I cannot believe either will sanction your disrespect of my clear desire not to be harassed by you."

"Harassed?" He chuckled. "You've not even been kissed."

Raúl moved his hands up under her wet hair. Despite her resistance, he kissed her thoroughly. When his lips lifted, his smile was gone. He drew an audible breath and released her, looking shaken.

"Just a hello," he mumbled. "Surely even you can't take offense." His voice strengthened. "Smile at me, sultry-voiced maiden. Admit you didn't find my greeting unpleasant."

She turned away, but he caught her hand.

"You must not miss out on life, Aurora. Only a *caballero* will do for you and I'm pleased to volunteer. I sense you'll be an apt pupil."

She jerked free of his grip and refused to meet his heated gaze. Her first kiss and he was only toying with her. Aurora sped across the grass as fast as dignity allowed.

He called after her, "I'll get into my boots and you into your dress, and we'll go home. An intriguing statement to anyone who did not witness our innocent encounter, *¿verdad?*"

She pulled her petticoat and dress over the soaked chemise. He'd spoiled her adventure. She could never come alone again to her perfect cove. She was tired of de Montaraz men. If not for Jocasta, she would leave tomorrow.

"Little sense in your walking in wet clothing. You'll ride with me." She was about to decline when he added, "Iván will know we were at the river whether we arrive together or apart."

What did he mean? The statement so distracted her that she allowed Raúl to lift her onto his horse. Resistance was probably futile, in any case. Cradled between his wet arms with his breath in her hair and his leather jacket about her shoulders, she escaped into prayer.

As they rode across the courtyard, Jocasta looked down from the balcony, shouting and waving to them. Don Iván stood with his daughter. He stared down with a narrowed gaze.

Aurora bit her lip. Don Iván would not want his brother involved with a servant. What if he sent her away? She didn't want to leave. Her relationship with Jocasta was precious.

Raúl called up, "The river was fine today. You two should have joined us."

As he lifted her from his horse, Aurora gritted her teeth. "Thank you, Don Raúl, for the company of a true gentleman."

He laughed at her acidic tone. "Until we meet again, enchantress."

"I'll see you at dinner, *preciosa*."

Iván waved as Luisa led Jocasta away, then stalked into his room. He paced the floor, finally pausing beneath the portraits of his parents. They'd hung in the library until he decided to bring Aurora into the house. He glared up at Don León's features, so like his daughter's.

"What were you thinking by asking us to bring her into the house?" Iván poured himself a small brandy and took a sip. He needed it.

Why was he upset? Look at things rationally. Raúl was following his usual pursuits. It didn't mean that Aurora was susceptible. Things being as they were, he had no right to interfere—if Raúl was serious.

Iván tried to dismiss the episode. He bathed and dressed for dinner and stepped onto his balcony once more, but even the beauty of the garden could not erase from his mind the picture of Aurora in Raúl's arms.

Nine

December 1807

Fall slid into winter. One December evening, Aurora walked hand in hand with Jocasta through the drought-damaged garden. The smell of smoke was stronger outside the house.

"Why won't Papá and my uncles come with us to the swing? I miss the good times."

Aurora cleared her scratchy throat. "I miss them, too, but the men are too tired."

The evening sessions with the men and Jocasta at the swing were now treasured memories. Aurora had felt a particular joy watching the little girl fly higher and higher. Raúl usually brought his guitar and his songs of the *rancho*. Don Iván seemed more relaxed, Raúl more respectful, and Jocasta accepting and eager to share her joy with Aurora, even if Justo was not.

Most of all, she missed smiles shared with Don Iván—the ones that made her heart rate increase.

Ridiculous reaction, but he seemed so accessible, watching her antics with his daughter. Those evenings were gone.

Autumn had failed to bring its usual rains. Each day dawned hotter and drier than the one before, turning December into late summer. Streams disappeared and even the river dwindled. Wildfires raged to the south of Rancho de Montaraz, and smoke hung in a cloying haze.

"The devil's breath," *indios* of the mission called the incessant winds. They brought temperatures as hot as those of the deserts where they originated, turning brush land into tinder.

The brothers de Montaraz, edgy and preoccupied at the breakfast table each morning, left to spend long days in the saddle. The men stood on constant alert while tending animals and patrolling pastures. They returned exhausted in late evening, more uncommunicative and withdrawn than ever.

"Drought and wildfire are not unknowns in the history of this ranch," Iván declared that evening at the dinner table. "But never a drought this severe. To the south, danger of fire often exists, but it now threatens the entire central coastline."

Jocasta piped up, "That will not happen here. Señorita Aurora and I pray for rain. God will hear us."

Don Iván patted her hand. "Your uncles and I are doing all we can. We will come through."

Aurora stared at him. *The skies are God's realm.*

If only he could assure Jocasta that he, too, was praying. Aside from Justo, she was uncertain of the men's faith. God's name was seldom on their lips. Elías followed the lead of Don Iván, and Raúl was Raúl.

Several hours after she tucked Jocasta in, the tower bell tolled and people shouted. A reddish glow stained the sky outside her window. Fire!

While pulling on her clothes, Aurora's bedroom door slammed open and Don Iván strode through. He barely glanced her direction.

"Dress warmly and follow me."

A prayer on her lips, she grabbed her jacket and slippers, not taking time for riding boots. She hurried into Jocasta's room where Luisa and María were dressing the little girl. Jocasta was still half-asleep.

Don Iván's strong hands reached for her. "Wake up, little one." He nuzzled her face to his. "We're going for a midnight ride."

Aurora picked up the doll at his feet. "We'll take Esperanza with us."

"Fire is near, isn't it, Papá?"

"Your uncles and the *vaqueros* protect the ranch. I will take both of you to a safe place the fire cannot reach, then return to help them." He grabbed a blanket and wrapped it around his daughter. "Bring one for yourself, Señorita."

Aurora had a hard time keeping up with his long strides down the stairs. She tried to slow her racing heart. It must be even more frightening for Jocasta, unable to see what was happening.

Servants hurried to and fro, loading valuables into wagons parked near the front door. Jorge followed outside to Don Iván's waiting stallion. He handed Jocasta up to her father, then helped Aurora mount behind Don Iván's saddle.

"Where is Corazón, Papa?"

"She's safe. *Tío* Elías moved the horses to safety."

"I will see to emptying the house and join you on the other side of the river." Jorge disappeared through the door.

Iván snuggled his daughter inside his fleece-lined cloak. He wheeled Diego toward the river. "Hold on tightly, Señorita."

Aurora clung to his cape. They overtook groups of women and children and another wagon before reaching a ford of the river.

"Dismount, Señorita, and wait for me here. I will return for you once I have Jocasta across."

Aurora wrapped the blanket around her, thankful for its warmth, and watched the horse ford the river. Even at low flow, water splashed up and covered Don Iván's boots.

She looked over her shoulder and cringed. The main house and outbuildings were silhouetted against a wall of fire consuming brush-covered hills to the southeast. Would it all be destroyed?

A pang of regret surprised her with its strength. She had once labeled the house a pretentious monument to wealth, but it was much more. It was precious to Jocasta, to Don Iván and his brothers—and to her. It had become her home.

Home had never been anything material to Aurora. It had been the love shared with her parents and her sister. The joy of meeting a loved one's need or in joined prayer at the end of a day. Now, home was where Jocasta was.

Hooves churned the river and Don Iván loomed beside her. Scooping her up with one arm, he gathered her to him and the blanket fell away. Opening his heavy cloak, he nestled her close to his chest, as he had Jocasta.

"I cannot allow you to ride behind me, Señorita. Your feet and legs would be wet and the night is cold. Hold onto me."

Aurora had never experienced the protective embrace of a man other than her father. Raúl's arms had controlled; Iván's comforted. His stubbly chin rubbed the top of her head as her arms circled his neck. A warm sense of security enveloped her inside the smoky cloak. She could ride forever in his strong arms.

He reined up and lowered her to the ground, his face inches from hers. She looked up at him as she slid down his booted leg, feeling her pulse in her throat. He stared at her for a long moment, then he and Diego vanished in a thunder of hooves.

She was setting herself up for heartbreak. He was her employer. Exasperating, opinionated, and accustomed to control. An aristocrat, and certainly not a man for the dreams of a simple governess. The night's drama was no excuse. He'd rescued her from danger and she was impressed by his strength and command of the situation, but she couldn't let it go further.

Aurora prayed for safety for the firefighters—and Iván. He could be Iván in her thoughts. He'd never know. She could maintain a proper balance. She must. He would send her away if he suspected.

She was doing a good job of keeping the balance with Raúl. He was problematic, but not beyond her ability to handle. She could do the same with her feelings for Iván.

Jorge arrived on his horse and the other servants in a wagon, laden with blankets, jugs of hot chocolate, coffee, and sandwiches. Jocasta ate heartily, and was soon asleep in Aurora's lap. Luisa and María drowsed nearby. In the distance, men shouted against the roar of the flames. Jorge paced the river bank, offering updates.

"The backfires are successful. The men have created firebreaks wide enough to prevent the wildfire reaching the house," he said at last.

After many tense hours, a male servant brought word it was safe to return. Transferring Jocasta to Jorge's arms, Aurora climbed into a wagon, then settled the little girl again in her lap. Jocasta reached up to put her arms around Aurora's neck and snuggled nearer under the blanket. Jorge mounted and galloped ahead.

"Don't leave me, Señorita Aurora. I don't ever want you to leave me." Jocasta's voice shook.

Tears sprang to Aurora's eyes. She never wanted to leave, but a governess had no control.

"I am here, Jocasta. You are safe."

"Is the house still there?" Jocasta murmured.

"Yes, darling, and we're going home. Everything will be all right." *Please, Holy Father, make it so.*

As the horses strained toward the house, Aurora could see small fires on the hills and hear distant shouts, but no flames threatened the great house or any of its dependencies. Some of the *vaqueros'* houses to the north were in the path of the only fire of any strength, and Aurora prayed again.

The front doors stood wide open and a commotion inside made her hold Jocasta more tightly. Jorge commanded the women to wait while he investigated. It was minutes before he returned. Iván was not with him. Her chest tightened. Where was he?

Jorge said, "María, you're needed in the main room. Men are injured. Luisa, please accompany Jocasta and the señorita to their rooms."

Without looking his way, Aurora said firmly, "Luisa, please take Jocasta. I will help María with the injured." She had to find Iván. Her hands trembled as she climbed from the wagon. She entered the house and spotted a tall figure standing in the middle of the foyer.

Praise God! He is safe!

Iván was directing Raúl and Elías and several workmen in setting up a makeshift hospital in the large *sala* just off the foyer.

Aurora approached his frown, heading off opposition with a question. "Where is Don Justo?"

"In his bedroom. One of his limbs is badly burned. Why are you not upstairs with Jocasta?" His face, blackened by smoke, looked forbidding.

"She is fine with Luisa. I'm here to help. I have experience as a nurse."

The frown deepened.

"His arm or his leg?"

Don Iván's eyes flashed irritation, but he answered, "His left leg."

She flushed as his reluctance became clear. In her concern, she'd breached proper conduct. Legs were not mentioned between ladies and gentlemen.

She followed him to Justo's bedroom, María in tow. Peeking under Iván's arm, Aurora glimpsed Justo writhing in agony as two footmen stripped away his clothing. The smell of smoke and burned flesh was alarming.

Iván blocked her view and pushed her gently into the hall. "Leave at once, Señorita. Please send Elías to me and we will tend our brother." He said to María, "Bring clean cloths and hot water."

Aurora caught her arm. "Send someone to

the mission at once for Pía and whichever doctor is available."

Don Iván's black gaze speared Aurora's, but he nodded. "A good idea. We need professionals. Since you insist on staying, Señorita, you may be able to help Raúl in the *sala*. Five men have burns."

She spent the next two hours cleansing burns and assessing which of the men were beyond her capabilities. There were two of them.

Raúl seemed to know what he was about. His actions were swift and gentle as they worked in tandem. With the help of Jorge, they moved the severely injured into a downstairs bedroom to await the doctor, offering strong doses of brandy as a pain killer. The burns of the remaining three Aurora and Raúl cleansed with strong tea and bandaged.

Raúl said to them, "You'll rest here overnight. We'll send word to your families. If all goes well, you can go home in the morning."

He turned to her. "Rest a while, Aurora. I'll watch them." His voice was gentle.

She shook her head. "One more urgent task. We need to pray for your family's praying man. Don Justo's injury is extensive. He could lose that limb."

Raúl's eyebrows lifted. "I've never been a praying man, but Iván said to follow your orders."

They knelt together in the middle of the room. One of the injured *vaqueros* called out, "The prayers of two or three together have great power. I will join you in praying to *El Señor*."

How these injured men needed God's mercy and healing. They needed Pía. As God's gifted nurse, she could offer both.

Ten

Aurora awoke, and pushed at the heavy blanket smothering her. She must have fallen asleep in her chair. Enough daylight filtered in to see the shapes of men on pallets in the *sala*. Raúl was nowhere in sight. Snores of the injured *vaqueros* rose and fell, almost masking voices in the entry hall.

Pía! Aurora pulled one of Jocasta's ribbons from her pocket, tied her hair back, smoothed her dress, and sped toward the foyer. She bumped into Jorge and a soldier heading for the kitchens.

Then she was in her sister's loving arms. The tightness in her chest drained. Pía was here.

Iván stood talking to a young man, who turned out to be Dr. Robles, and nearby stood Pía's assistant, Genevra.

"Our patients, Aurora," Pía said, rolling up her sleeves and picking up her reticule. "Take me to them."

The brothers led the doctor and Genevra toward Justo's bedside, and Aurora took Pía to the room that held the most critically injured *vaqueros*. María brought clean linens, and Jorge lugged in a cauldron of steaming water. He didn't stay, saying Don Iván had another errand for him.

In a short time, Pía had examined the men's burns and was ready with her assessment. "We must cleanse the bodies of these men before we attempt treatment. More hot water, María, several additional basins. Clean cloths—"

"Not a woman's task. My brother and I will see to it. Take your sister to the arboretum, Señorita Aurora, until I send for you." Aurora didn't notice Iván's return until he stepped between her and the injured men, a wall not to be breached.

Pía stiffened and her black eyes flashed. "Please do not hinder my work, Señor de Montaraz. Trained nurses must perform the baths. First hours are critical."

Aurora intervened. "She is an exceptional nurse, Don Iván."

Iván's face turned to stone. He refused to budge when Pía attempted to push past. A staring contest was broken by Raúl's snort of laughter behind Aurora.

"Brother, one professional nurse outranks two untrained men." His grin showed how much he enjoyed watching his formidable brother bested by a small Indian woman.

Iván turned on his heel, followed by Raúl. Pía seemed unaffected by the men's abrupt departure, focused as she was on requirements of bathing the men.

Aurora helped Pía and María strip off the men's filthy clothing. When their bodies had been washed, Pía added the contents of several vials to a steaming cauldron and dipped water into basins. The men looked uneasy, as if fearing another painful cleansing.

"We'll cleanse the wounds again, then apply linseed oil and lime water. After that, a balm of honey and aloe, dried plantain, and calendula. You can help me by crushing the dried plants. I've found the treatment very effective." Pía turned to María. "Please find enough clean linen sheets to swathe their entire bodies." She began unpacking containers of the herbs she needed, along with her mortar and pestle.

Aurora began grinding the plants. "Seeing these unimpressive weeds growing in the wild I never imagined they had medicinal uses. Aloe, of course, I know to be soothing in any burn."

"My mother's people have deep medicinal wisdom that Spanish doctors ignore. Their patients suffer. They sniff at my remedies until they see their effectiveness."

Midday rainbows danced in the foyer as Aurora and Pía made their way to Justo's room hours later. The doctor stood outside the sickroom surrounded by the brothers. Their grim faces showed the news could not be good. As the women neared, the doctor, Raúl, and Elías returned to Justo's room.

Aurora's heart went out to Iván. He'd replaced his smoke-blackened clothing with a fresh suit and shaved, but he looked exhausted. He stared at his feet, a tall, stalwart figure in distress.

She remembered a cypress she had once seen at the edge of a cliff. Beset by a gale from the sea, it bent so low she thought it would be ripped from the earth, but its roots were deep and strong. Iván, too, would weather the storm. It was his duty.

"What did the doctor say about Justo?" Aurora held her breath.

"The limb must come off. He says we cannot risk infection from such a massive burn." His voice was toneless.

Aurora gasped and glanced at Pía, whose expression remained unchanged.

"I want to see him, Don Iván. Please allow me to examine your brother." Pía's voice was firm.

Iván rubbed at his eyes. They must still smart from hours of exposure to smoke. "I cannot see what that will accomplish, Señorita, except to horrify you. The wound is extensive."

Aurora wanted to caution Pía. She looked ready to do battle again. What if Iván sent her sister away?

"There are often alternatives to surgery," Pía snapped, "if only these learned men would try. This young doctor is fresh from medical school in Europe where the first line of defense is to cut. They cut away anything that might require long and uncertain treatment." She looked steadily at Iván. "I want to try to save the limb. My mother's people had curatives unknown to Spanish doctors. Effective ones."

Iván raked a hand through his hair and slumped onto a hall bench. "I am reluctant to go against the advice of a professional." He controlled his voice, but it was clear Pía's words were an unwelcome complication. "The doctor says his life can be forfeited in a matter of hours if blood poisoning sets in."

Pía seemed to weigh his words, nodding. "True. There is always a risk. Is Don Justo conscious? Perhaps he should make the decision."

She was right. Aurora touched Iván's arm.

"Would you not want to be consulted if the limb were your own? Pía is a nurse of experience. Please let her at least examine your brother before it is too late. God leads her."

Iván came to life. He uttered a growl and jumped to his feet. He paced up and down the hallway for several minutes, hands locked behind his back. Had Pía's opposition pushed him too far? His expression yielded none of his thoughts when he faced them.

"Very well, ladies. Your reasoning is sound. Justo should have a say. Señorita Pía may examine him, but you, Señorita Aurora, will return to Jocasta. You have been away from your charge long enough." His expression softened. "And you must be very tired. Have Luisa pour you a hot bath and bring food." He strode into Justo's bedroom, Pía on his heels.

Late afternoon light was a golden haze outside the glass doors of Aurora's study. She could hear Jocasta and Luisa on the balcony. She lifted a pot of gently weakened tea toward Pía's waiting cup.

"Drink, baby sister, and have more to eat. Don Iván says the danger of fire has passed. His men successfully beat it down, though at fearful cost. So many injured."

"I'm sure his judgment can be trusted in any ranch matter. In others, I'm not so certain. He holds a narrow judgment of what women can accomplish."

Aurora nodded. "As do most men. I sometimes think only our Savior and the friars know how strong we are." She gestured toward a plate half-filled with toasted sandwiches, but Pía shook her head.

"Don Iván is an honorable man, Pía. A loving father, and a very fair employer. Inflexible, but a good man. He has a problem with trust. Admits to it freely."

Pía sipped her tea. "Genevra stayed, but the learned doctor left in a huff when his advice was ignored."

"What are Justo's chances? Can the leg be saved?"

"Certainty belongs only to God, but I've seen wounds of the same magnitude respond to conservative treatment. A man with one leg in the wilds of California is a disadvantaged creature. Don Justo, in a coherent moment, thanked me for trying. He's committed to doing exactly as I tell him."

She sighed and set her cup aside. "I'll bathe and rest for a couple of hours before I return to his bedside. Pray without ceasing, sister." She moved toward the door, ready for the next task.

Aurora nodded and slipped to her knees. If Justo died, Iván might never forgive them; but Pía was right to try.

Across the landing in his suite of rooms, Iván paced. What had he done? Was the judgment—no, the faith—of two young women to be trusted? This whole matter with Aurora was getting out of hand.

He glanced up at his father's portrait. Father's cool logic had served him well over the years. Men of reason traded in facts. Religion ranked with superstition, and a rational man did not entertain either.

Why had he abandoned the habit of a lifetime? In his distress he allowed himself to indulge the earnest pleas of Aurora and her sister. What was there about

Aurora that he found so compelling if not her faith? He had developed a dangerous soft spot where she was concerned.

Acknowledging that rest was impossible, Iván returned to his brother's room to relieve Raúl. Pía entered a short time later and they shared a silent bedside vigil. Hours passed, but she did not sleep.

What was going through this woman's mind? Her face was devoid of expression, and her gaze would briefly meet his, but she seemed to feel no need for words. Occasionally, she rose and bent over Justo to offer water or to remove a dressing. She'd smear some concoction on a clean cloth and rewrap the wound. Then she'd return to her chair. At times she bowed her head. Was she praying?

Aurora would have been. It seemed she prayed about everything. Her head would bow and her eyes close. After moments she'd rejoin her surroundings with no explanation, but he knew she'd been praying.

Pía's compassion had an edge of steel. Aurora was much softer in her discipline. But he recognized if she drew a line, nothing he could do would persuade her to change course. She would follow what she believed was God's guidance. She had won Jocasta with barely a clash of wills, but Pía seemed not to care whose egos she bruised if the good of her patient was concerned.

Unfathomable women. The sisters obviously shared a mindset that they felt needed no explanation. The idea of asking for guidance both attracted and repelled him. It would be comforting to believe in wisdom greater than his, but experience told him he was on his own.

During the next few days Aurora worried almost as much about her sister as she did about Justo. Pía appeared indefatigable, but Aurora knew how many hours she spent on her feet, looking after her patients. Baths, dressing changes, coaxing cranky men to eat—the chores were endless.

Justo and one *vaquero* remained the most critical after five days. The *vaquero's* lungs were seared and Justo's leg remained agonizingly unhealed. Genevra spent most of her time with him.

Aurora did what she could, and the brothers took turns supervising ranching operations and sitting with Justo. Pía abided by a strict schedule, insisting that Aurora and Genevra do the same. They must have rest and proper nutrition.

"What good will it do if we ourselves grow sick? Off with you, Aurora. Rest now. You have your duties with Jocasta as well as tending these men."

Dinners were strained affairs, but Pía appeared oblivious to the censorious presence at the head of the table. Each evening was a repetition of the one before. Iván sat withdrawn, his eyes black and brooding after questioning Pía about Justo's progress in the past twenty-four hours.

"The healing of burns can be a long process. Don Justo's condition could go either way. I see no tell-tale red streaks of infection, but the wound needs scrupulous care and I offer my best. The outcome is in God's hands, Don Iván."

He seemed dissatisfied with her answers, but Aurora knew Pía would never offer unwarranted reassurance. Iván's attitude was disappointing. If only he had the solace of prayer.

There were no formal dinner prayers until the third evening when Jocasta said, "*Tío* Justo would want us to pray." She stood, offered thanks for the meal, and prayed for the recovery of her beloved uncle. The brothers looked a little shamed. They waited each evening thereafter for Jocasta's blessing.

Raúl took over the role of host in Iván's silent abdication. He turned his considerable charm on Pía and kept conversations far removed from the sickrooms. One evening after causing Pía to laugh, his merry glance caught Aurora's uneasy one. He offered a cheeky smile and wagged two playful fingers.

"You sisters are equally beautiful and charming, but Pía seems to appreciate me more than you do, Señorita Aurora."

Iván glowered. "Inappropriate, Raúl."

His brother's disapproval did nothing to dampen Raúl's spirits. He and Pía shared watches at Don Justo's bedside. What did he say when they were alone?

Pía had no experience with men. Was she vulnerable to the smiles and flattery of the handsome ladies' man? She said he spent hours with his brother, showing an innate sense of what was needed. What else did she appreciate about Raúl?

Eleven

February 1808

At the end of the week Aurora took a midnight watch and Raúl joined her. The painkilling drugs kept Justo's suffering to a minimum, but he was often incoherent, unable to recognize anyone. They watched Justo toss in his sleep until he struggled to sit up.

"Water. I need water."

Aurora lifted a glass to his lips.

His eyes focused on her face and he hissed, "What are you doing here? Where is Nurse Pía?"

She gasped and her hand trembled. Raúl took the glass.

"Señorita Aurora is allowing her sister to rest by staying with you. She has been most kind to you."

"I do not want her here."

The words were slurred, but Justo's gaze was clear and cold. He knew exactly what he said. Aurora was grateful for his improved condition, but his hostility tied a knot in her stomach.

Raúl squeezed her shoulder. "Go rest, Aurora. I'll stay with this cranky bear."

She fled to her quarters, pausing only to check on the other injured man and Genevra. As she neared the top of the stairs, she murmured, "Don Justo despises me for no apparent reason. Why do these men resent me?"

A deep voice startled her. "My brother is ill. Please do not think badly of him—of all of us. We can be complicated creatures, it seems."

"I have a strange habit of speaking thoughts aloud, Don Iván. Is Jocasta all right?"

He reached for the candle she carried and they crossed the landing.

"You must have felt much alone until the coming of your sister. Good that you have her, despite sad circumstances. In answer to your question, Jocasta is sleeping peacefully; and I noted this evening that my brother is healing with his limb intact. Thank you, Señorita, for standing strong. Sleep well." He turned away.

Aurora reached for the door handle, then paused. "Don Iván, please give me a moment. It is more than illness that causes Don Justo's resentment. I have sensed resistance in all of you from the start. Will you help me understand?"

"We are not trusting men, but we don't oppose you, Señorita. You are doing good work with Jocasta." His voice was soft, reassuring.

Aurora felt the effort of her shrug. She wanted him to see her dissatisfaction. If Iván thought she accepted his glib answer, he was mistaken. There was something more, and she meant to learn the truth.

Four days later, Pía was ready to return to her duties at the mission, saying Don Justo would mend without her. Iván insisted she accept a generous number of gold coins in payment for her services.

"All I want is your permission for Aurora to spend Christmas at the mission. The good Fray Peralta joins me in the request."

Iván agreed, and Raúl and Elías drove off with Pía and Genevra in an open carriage. Aurora and Jocasta stood with Don Iván on the veranda.

Jocasta called a final goodbye and waved. "I like her, Señorita Aurora. I like your sister, but I am a little frightened of her."

Aurora put an arm around the girl. "You don't fear her, *preciosa*. You respect her. Respect is a good thing and Señorita Pía deserves it."

"A true statement. Both sisters deserve respect." Iván smiled the smile that made Aurora's heart beat lose its rhythm.

Before she left the ranch for her holiday at the mission, rains came. For three days it rained so hard Aurora had to delay her trip. She clasped her hands in prayer and counted blessings. The drought was broken; Justo walked with the aid of a crutch; the *vaquero* with the seared lung had moved back to the care of his wife; and Jocasta offered a kiss as Aurora departed.

"Just what I needed," Aurora said to Pía after the first night's mass. "A time of restoration and worship." The voices of Indian children lifted in praise worked their magic, and the ceremony brought alive once again the majesty of God. "Holy Days with you and Fray Peralta, and other dear ones of the mission. You strengthen my faith."

The talk turned to Jocasta and Pía said, "You love the child as a mother."

Fray Peralta nodded. "You've become her spiritual mother. Quite possibly your faith will have an effect on her father and his brothers."

Aurora shook her head. "I see nothing of the sort. My prayers in that direction have borne no fruit."

Fray Peralta nodded. "All in God's time. He alone changes hearts."

"Listen to him, Aurora. Because of Fray Peralta's counsel I have become the woman God intended. At sixteen, I believed I should go to the convent in Mexico City. But he helped me see that I was already doing the work of Christ at the mission among the poor and needy, the lame and the blind, so dear to the heart of our Savior. It would have been wrong to leave my work with the sick and take up the sequestered life I thought I wanted."

"Oh, yes, Pía. You are doing the work God intended and have found satisfaction. I thought the mission schoolroom was my calling, but now I am not so certain. I have become very fond of Jocasta. I find both challenge and satisfaction at Rancho de Montaraz. I have come to think of it as my home, although it will not be a permanent one."

"Raúl came again yesterday," Pía said. "He promised to return soon, and said Justo will visit us as soon as he is able."

"Raúl and Justo? Do you not use their titles?"

"Friends don't need titles. They both call me Pía. After all, I'm a simple Indian nurse. I shared with them some intimate moments. It's a part of my calling, and I don't shrink from necessity."

Aurora avoided her gaze and stroked the crucifix at her throat. Justo was a safer option. Should she warn Pía of Raúl's womanizing reputation? Her chin lowered to her chest. Who was she to give advice?

This time Pia could not count on the advice of her older sister. Aurora's impossible heart flutters around Iván proved she had no wisdom. He was not the man for her. Not that she didn't want him; she did. But he was beyond her reach.

Did God have a man in mind for her? If not, she could dedicate herself to His work among children and find a fulfilling life. When Jocasta no longer needed her, there would be others.

At the breakfast table two weeks after Aurora's return from the mission, Justo said, "I'm fit for work." Her heart celebrated. She and Jocasta could return to normal routines. For days he had roamed the hacienda on his crutch and disrupted school hours, demanding that Jocasta stay at his side.

Iván, on the other hand, surprised and delighted her with a much-relaxed attitude. He had become a willing partner in Jocasta's education. Several times he'd come to the classroom with displays for the nature table, and once with a trunk filled with clothing of his ancestors. He'd insisted Aurora wear one of the magnificent dresses to dinner, much to Justo's displeasure. Aurora's heart sang and she felt at ease with the world during the rides she and Jocasta shared with Iván.

Raúl felt slighted, she knew. He grumbled, "I invite you time after time and you say it would be inappropriate. How is it different to ride with my brother? Perhaps I should ask Pía."

No explanation sufficed. The ladies' man was obviously unused to rejection. Raúl could not truly care for her; he didn't want to see Iván succeed where he could not. She would offer him no more. Aurora had been clear from the outset that she did not want to factor into the men's lives. Iván would not want anything more from an employee.

Winter had been a typical mix of rainy and sunny days. From the schoolroom, Aurora and Jocasta heard the brothers come in the front entry one blustery February afternoon.

"I must speak to my uncle." Jocasta took Aurora's hand and pulled her toward the railing of the upstairs balcony. "*Tío,*" she called down. "*Tio* Elías. Please come up. I need you."

Iván's tall figure stood out in the rainbow dance of afternoon sunlight, his cape thrown back to show its fleecy lining. Jorge took it, and moved toward the others who were loosening their own cloaks. Iván raised his face to stare up at Aurora for a moment, but her smile went unanswered. He broke from the group and strode toward his office.

"Coming," Elías answered. His iron spurs rang on the stone steps. He reached a bench, and sat down to unbuckle them from his boots.

"What I can do for my favorite little lady?"

"Take me into the garden and help me gather dried plants. Señorita Aurora says I'm ready to create bouquets without her, but I'll need your eyes for the prickles."

"We'll go at once." Elías winked at Aurora.

"We'll need a mix of grasses and twigs, *Tío*. I'll show you how to arrange them, the tallest in the center."

Elías' amused eyes met Aurora's. "I see I'm in the hands of a professional." Jocasta beamed and Elías reached for her small hand to descend the treacherous stairs.

Aurora cleaned up after the efforts of a busy soon-to-be-five-year-old and laid out materials for the following day. Her heart beat faster.

She'd share another of Jocasta's achievements with Iván and watch his eyes glow with approval. She could bask in his heart-stopping smile. Every fiber of her being felt involved when he smiled that way, warmed as if he'd offered the highest praise.

Aurora crossed the foyer a few minutes later, Jocasta's watercolor in her hands. She would suggest it be framed and hung in the breakfast room for the family to enjoy.

The painting had been inspired by a brilliant sunset the previous evening. The strength of the sun's light made its splendor visible even to Jocasta's veiled eyes, and her sweet voice had risen in a song of thanks to God. Don Iván's gaze had found Aurora's and he'd nodded approval.

She knocked on the office door.

"*Adelante*."

Aurora pushed the heavy door closed behind her.

Light streamed through stained glass behind the desk, creating a rainbow of earth-toned patterns on the floor. It was the only thing she could relate to in the masculine room. Heavy bookcases, a massive mahogany desk and chair, and the immense stone fireplace: it was a fitting domain for the director of an empire.

Iván stood, his back to her, with one hand on the mantel, his powerful shoulders hunched forward as he stared into the blaze. A brandy snifter on the mantel held the remains of a drink.

"Don Iván?" He didn't turn.

Aurora held out the watercolor. "Jocasta completed this painting today, all on her own. It shows such promise. I could not wait to share it with you—" Her voice trailed away as he continued to stare into the flames.

He was still in his boots and work clothes. His gloves, hat, and spurs on the corner of the desk offered mute testimony that he'd remained in the office since she'd seen him an hour ago. The strong shadow of a beard marked his face and his black hair hung in disarray. He'd been raking his hand through it. She knew the gesture. He was disturbed.

"I am sorry to have intruded. We can talk later."

He raised his head and something in his eyes made her step back. A quiver went through her. With a groan, he reached out and pulled her hard against him.

Twelve

Cupping the back of her head, Iván brought her lips to his. "Aurora," he moaned. He tasted of brandy and smelled of leather and the outdoors. His beard roughened her face as he kissed her again and again.

When her initial shock gave way, Aurora stood on the tips of her toes and held onto him with all her strength, transported into his desire as the kisses continued.

"Oh, Iván," she whispered against his lips. "I didn't know you felt what I've been afraid to acknowledge in myself. I thought you a man of whom I dared not dream." For the first time she used the intimate Spanish *tú*.

His breath was in her hair. His lips brushed the shell of her ear and she shivered. Iván lifted her into his arms.

"Do I frighten you, *preciosa*? You're trembling." His voice was soft as his black eyes searched hers.

"No, Iván. It must be excitement." Aurora closed her eyes, recognizing the truth of her words. She remembered how intimidating his appearance had once been. His size and strength and his intensity. No longer. Beneath his ardor, she sensed great tenderness.

He stepped toward a leather sofa fronting the fireplace, laid her there, and knelt beside her. Hungry kisses at last gave way to touches like the brush of a feather. His fingers swept lightly along a cheekbone, swooped down the line of her nose, and lingered along her lip as he gently kissed each spot. "Smooth cheeks, sweet little nose, and lips—your delectable lips. I worship them all," he whispered.

Aurora's eyes were glued shut by feelings so new and enthralling. She wanted the kisses never to end. He loved her. This astonishing man loved her.

At last she opened her eyes. She thought he'd arise and pull her up, but his attention was riveted on her neck. He reached out a long finger and touched a blood vessel pulsing beneath her ear. It seemed to hold him on his knees, mesmerized.

His fingers caressed the edges of her ear and his eyes darkened. She watched his lids grow heavy. His kiss was hungry again on her throat and her mouth. She closed her eyes, reveling in his touch.

I could not have imagined. Not even in a dream. Never.

"Aurora," he whispered, "open your eyes and look at me."

"Mmmm?"

"Look at me, *querida*. I want to make you mine. I need you desperately."

Iván's insistent words finally registered. Aurora dragged her eyes open. He had raised his lips from hers, but they remained inches away. She felt warm and lethargic. He was irresistible. She could drown in those black eyes.

She closed her own again when she could no longer bear the intensity of his. She felt his hands at the bodice of her dress.

Aurora forced her eyes open. She caught at his hands and he jerked them back, as if he'd been scalded. His face was taut and flushed.

"You've done nothing wrong, Iván." She touched his hair, feeling a little shy. Her fingers sifted its coarseness. "Can you sense how much I love you? I want you to make love to me more than I ever thought possible."

Not a muscle moved in his face. She put her hand to his cheek and whispered, "But, *mi amor,* I want it to be after we're married. I want us to follow God's plan for a man and a woman who love one another as we do. Our joy must be consecrated to Him. Do you understand what I'm saying?"

He pulled her upright into his arms and stroked back her hair. He kissed her forehead. "I do understand. I had no right to ask. I lost control, Aurora. I vowed I would never put you in this position, but I lost control!"

His expression was raw, his eyes tormented by something she couldn't fathom. He sounded angry. "Forgive me if you can." Iván released her.

She swayed on her feet, shocked and bereft. She reached for his arm to steady herself. Iron beneath her fingers. Her heart pounded and her scalp prickled. What was wrong?

"Iván, there's nothing to forgive. You've made me happy beyond my wildest dreams. I ache to share in the fulfillment of our love. What can you mean?"

He pulled her into a crushing embrace and

buried his face in her hair. Several agonizing moments passed before he growled, "There can be no marriage, Aurora. I had no right to give in to my feelings with such knowledge. Can you forgive me?"

"What do you mean there can be no marriage? Why can't you marry me?"

He didn't answer, holding her tighter and kissing the top of her head.

"Answer me, Iván." She pushed back in his arms. "Do you mean you *will* not marry me? I have no dowry, but surely a rich man does not need to add to his fortune. What possible reason can you offer?" She struggled against his strength.

"¡*Sueltame!* Let go of me!" Aurora pushed free of his embrace. "Face me. Look into my eyes and say you will not marry me."

He froze, his expression shuttered against her. He didn't speak.

"Your patrician pride? Can you not force yourself to marry the daughter of a *vaquero*? An honorable man who served this very ranch? True, I'm of mixed ancestry, but my mother came from a good enough family to satisfy even the elevated notions of landed Castilians. It must be my father's low estate that gets up your proud nose."F

Black mirrors reflected her shocked face. Iván's breath came hard and his mouth formed a grim line, but not a word emerged.

"A servant is fitting to take as a lover, but not as wife for the son of León de Montaraz? Answer me."

His hand shot out and gripped her arm. His face inches from hers, he growled, "Look at me, Aurora." He spaced the words. "Do you see the patrician features of a Castilian? My black hair. My large hands. My dark skin. Do you see an aristocrat?"

Her arm throbbed. Aurora could not speak. What was he saying?

"I'm the bastard son of one of the soldiers of the mission. My mother was an Indian. I and my brothers are the adopted sons of the noble León de Montaraz and his wife Juliana. True sons of the countryside. No heritage except what two kind people saw fit to offer four orphans. I have no other claim to pride."

Aurora trembled in the face of his intensity. He dropped her arm and turned to the fire once more. Hand again outstretched to the mantel, his body rigid, he stared again into the flames.

With his release Aurora felt she might collapse. Her legs were jelly. Her arm ached from his grip. She wanted to crawl away, but she had to know.

"Then I really do not understand. I wouldn't have dared dream you might love me if you'd not given me that vision in your arms. You're the one who stirred the embers; you must throw water on the ashes. Tell me, Iván! What is wrong with me that you cannot marry me? I have a right to explanation."

Iván's troubled gaze met hers. He shook his head. "Forget this ever happened. I do not for a moment suppose you can forgive me, but I ask you to believe me when I say there can be no marriage. I lost control, Aurora—I lost control. I did not intend to insult you." He had returned to formal Spanish terms.

The realization hurt. "Forget? How can I forget? Living in the same house. Seeing you every day."

He shook his head. "I will stay out of your sight as much as I can."

"You did not claim to love me, only that you wanted me and needed me; but I sensed something deeper. Are you saying it was the passion of a man and nothing more? Do you have no true feeling for me?"

He refused to look at her, his fists clenched as he stared into the fire. "You must not leave this house, Aurora. Stay. You have the right, even if you now despise me."

The command of master to servant. Aurora trembled with fury. Her legs shook so hard she thought they might give way.

"Leave? How can I leave the child who owns half my heart? Do you know nothing of the woman for whom you professed such passion only moments ago?"

He wouldn't look at her. She goaded him. "I cannot be so self-concerned as to leave her to the care of reckless men who have no wisdom for her. No understanding of selfless love. I will never leave her unless you bodily throw me out of this house."

Iván looked desperate. To offer things unsaid? His lips moved and she took hope, but all that came from him was a ragged breath. His mouth twisted. His hand reached out, then fell to his side. She watched him turn to stone, his black eyes gleaming and unfathomable. He turned away, his brooding gaze once again on the flames.

Hopeless. "As you say, Iván, it is best you stay away from me. Tell Raúl to do the same. Adopted sons or no, none of the de Montaraz men should be molesting a paid servant with their attentions."

She stooped to pick up the crumpled watercolor, which had been crushed between them. She smoothed it against the stone of the fireplace. Thrusting it into his hands, Aurora whirled and stalked from the room. She did not look back as she closed the door behind her on her moments of joy, now as dead as she felt. She forced her wooden legs to climb the stairs.

Iván took two long strides toward the door and stopped. Raking a hand through his hair, he uttered an oath. How could he have been so reckless? So stupid?

He'd maintained discipline all his well-ordered life. One unguarded moment and he was swept away like a stick in a stream. He'd lost control. Lost everything.

His face stiff with anguish, he returned to the decanter and lifted its amber weight in his hand. He stared at the remaining brandy, wanting to blame it for his debacle, then set it down. It would not help the pain, and he needed to remain in control.

Aurora, Aurora. Why didn't I tell you truth at the outset? What will I do now?

Thirteen

An owl hooted its night cry in the distance. Nearby, a dove called, low and forlorn. Desolate echoes of Aurora's troubled night.

At the rail of her balcony, she stood watching stars fade into the brilliant turquoise of dawn. Escaping the torture of her bed had not ended the torment. Its claws had sunk deep into her mind. No relief in the promise of a new day.

In the garden below a twig snapped beneath a heavy footfall. She leaned over and caught her breath. Iván looked up at her from the shadowed courtyard, his face caught in a torch's glow. He stared up at her in the moment before Aurora turned and fled to her room.

Colors fused, amber and pink, as sunlight painted the ceiling. She washed and dressed, but made no move to waken Jocasta. Luisa came to see why the two had not come down.

"We'll breakfast on the balcony when Jocasta wakens. I'm sure Don Iván will understand. There may be similar mornings. If we plan to eat with the men, we'll arrive at the usual time. There's no need to check on us each morning."

"But, Señori—"

"I plan to use our private breakfasts to introduce new foods. Jocasta doesn't need meat and eggs every morning like those hard-working men. We'll try cereal and fruits this morning. I'll ring when we're ready."

Her hands shook and her eyes were gritty. The night had been long. Painful. Anger sustained her through the first sleepless hour. At the end of the second, Aurora repositioned her pillow again, but emotions swelled, refusing to be released. Her chest had ached with unshed tears.

She'd known. She knew from her mother's experience. Aristocrats lived in a world of their own. She could expect nothing from him.

Then Iván took her into his arms.

Like a ribbon removed from her long braid, the scene of last evening unfurled, shredding her senses. She tried giving a name to her anguish.

Loss? Sadness? A distillation of the two. What she felt was grief—the irrevocable change of expectations. She could deal with it. She'd dealt with grief at the deaths of her parents.

Turn to prayer. Expose it before God. But no words came. The anguish remained. Consuming. Overwhelming.

Early in their acquaintance she'd responded to Iván's brooding good looks and his long, lithe stride. Her eyes had followed him for months. Watching. Admiring. He'd fascinated her, but she was unsure when her feelings deepened.

Had he ever known personal defeat? His

certainty was not arrogance, as she'd first suspected. It was confidence. He knew his way and followed it. His mission was to preserve the hacienda and the relationship between the brothers. Accustomed to his carefully-reasoned words, the recent moments of unrestrained laughter he'd shared with her and Jocasta had caught her in delight.

Of all the qualities that drew her, one prevailed: Iván's delight in Jocasta's development. A bond had formed between them. Something in his love for Jocasta bound her heart to his. Something that showed on his face and in his eyes when he looked at his daughter. Something strong that held onto a woman's heart. A love she could count on.

She whispered a shamed confession to the only One who would understand. In her anger she had accused Iván of being unable to give the very thing which drew her: love that expected no reward.

"He understands sacrificial love, Father. He wants the good of Jocasta more than he wants his own. Love solid enough to encompass a woman's needs along with those of his daughter. When Iván finds the right woman for him and to mother his child, he will give her unswerving devotion. I'm not that woman, but I long to be."

None of it mattered. She couldn't stop loving him any more than she could stop the sun from rising. The thought haunted her, a weight that pressed into her soul. She could not carry it alone.

She needed Pía beside her. Her sister's steady faith always strengthened her; but Pía was far down the coast at Mission San Antonio, where there had been an outbreak of some disease.

I cannot go running to Fray Peralta. I must face this on my own.

A sob rose in her throat and she whispered, "I must learn to give Iván de Montaraz into Your loving hands, Holy Father, and not seek to satisfy either my longings or his desires."

Her heartbeat felt sluggish, seeming to find its rhythm difficult. She could still feel Iván's arms around her, his lips on hers. Her reverie shattered as Jocasta called out.

The little girl was a warm, sleepy hump of rumpled nightclothes and tangled covers. Aurora hugged her and they prayed for the new day and each person dear to their hearts.

Jocasta customarily sent up sweet and trusting prayers for her father and each of the uncles she treasured. Only recently had she added prayers for Aurora before the ones for the horses and whatever orphan animal the barnyard held.

At the sight of breakfast on a silver tray, Jocasta clapped her hands and squealed. "What is on the tray, Señorita Aurora?"

"A cinnamon stick in each cup ready to lend its spicy richness to hot chocolate I'll pour from a fat pot. You have hot cereal with apple slices and thick cream. A breakfast fit for a princess."

Jocasta adored sweets, but Aurora limited them. It had been a bone of contention between the two early on, but Don Iván backed Aurora and praised his daughter's widening palate.

The little girl attacked her breakfast as Aurora picked at hers, planning further adjustments. She must try to avoid Iván whenever possible. No trips to the orchard or horseback rides and picnics with father and daughter. Breakfasts would be fairly easy to change, but family dinners were another matter. There'd be no avoiding dinner with the men on most nights.

How could she adjust to being once again the unwelcome guest?

God's grace is sufficient. Words her parents and Fray Peralta lived by. He'd chosen her to bring Jocasta closer to Him and she would honor the call. Whatever existed between her and Iván could not be as important as God's plan. She would not crumple under the weight of emotions.

The day inched by and Aurora reminded herself many times of God's presence. She tried to bury her grief in the routine of studies, a light meal in early afternoon, and a foray into the garden to examine the butterfly chrysalis they'd watched for weeks.

Jocasta's bright chatter was balm, and once when the little lump of love kissed her cheek, Aurora thought her aching heart might heal. Her sweet hugs and occasional kiss, her laughter, and the moments of discovery they shared would be enough. Jocasta made staying at Rancho de Montaraz imperative.

Aurora rubbed her aching temples. Iván had ordered her to stay; he must recognize her worth in his daughter's life. Surely he would put the good of Jocasta before his aversion to continued employment of a woman he desired, but would not marry. He'd be able to carry off an uncomfortable situation.

Or would he send her away as an unwelcome temptation?

"May we take our new arrangement downstairs, Señorita Aurora?" Jocasta added, "I hear my *caballeros*. We can catch them before they dress for dinner."

Today's arrangement was a triumph of flowers, seed pods, and grasses collected and preserved the past summer. Aurora carried the heavy arrangement as María helped Jocasta down the stairs and continued on toward the kitchen.

A fire glowed in the conservatory and the smell of rich, humid soil was so strong it caught in Aurora's throat. With a hammering heart, she braced herself to meet the eyes of Iván de Montaraz, finally casting a cautious peep at the men standing near the fire. Iván was not with his brothers. Her chest felt lighter.

Elías hugged Jocasta and beamed at Aurora. Raúl bowed low and offered a knowing smirk. Justo immediately took the arrangement from Aurora's hands, and asked Jocasta to help him put it in its proper place.

Aurora tried to excuse herself, but Raúl held out a glass. "Welcome to our little nun. A cool drink? Even the most saintly can enjoy a juice drink before dinner. No alcohol. No fear of loosening the restraints of virginal innocence." His voice was bitter—challenging.

Why the hostility? Raúl had returned to his old, taunting manner. She sank into the leathery embrace of a broad-shouldered armchair next to Elías, and reached for the glass, determined to show good grace.

"Thank you, Don Raúl." She took a sip. "Delicious."

Elías took a seat and Raúl sprawled into a chair across from her. He raked her with his eyes. "Do you see yourself entering a convent someday?"

What was this about? Raúl had been much kinder and helpful in recent weeks. He'd even brought a heavy tree limb to the school room and stayed to place the empty nests just so. Surely Iván would not have told him what happened last evening.

"No, Don Raúl, I have never felt such a call."

He examined her from head to toe. "Excellent discernment on your part. A waste of womanly attributes, to hide yourself away from the eyes of men."

Elías' eyes blazed and he burst out, "Raúl, there's no call for you to show disrespect. We all resent your insolence, even Justo." He set his drink down, as if preparing to rise.

Raúl threw up his hands. "Whoa, little brother. She needs no defense. It's a game we play, both of us willing participants. Aurora said she brought no weapons into our house, but she is formidably armed. Look at her. Her fighting equipment gives her a strong edge over a helplessly admiring man. I'm a pawn in her beautiful hands."

Raúl's gaze continued to move slowly over her body as he spoke.

Aurora tamped down the heat rising inside her. Ignore his attempts to draw her into a scene. She turned to Elías. "Please don't allow bad feelings to flare because of me. I've learned to ignore Don Raúl's more unwelcome attentions, and to be grateful for the times when he seems genuinely helpful."

Raúl's eyes narrowed. "Well spoken, Señorita. The perfect parry." His voice was icy.

Whatever was wrong, the problem was his. Hers was how to survive a family dinner. She took another sip of her drink; then arose with a nod to Raúl and a smile for Elías. The youngest brother's chiding voice rose again as she reached the door.

Fourteen

Aurora's hands shook. She finally allowed María to finish placing the combs in her hair. Her brave resolutions had faltered when the actual time neared for dinner with the men. She stared at her image in the mirror and pinched her pale cheeks.

I am God's woman. He will guide me.

She refused to rehearse what she must do or say when she faced Iván. What if he told her to leave, despite his words of last night? Now that he'd had time to brood on her harsh words, he may have decided she was not the woman to mold his daughter. She would never see him or Jocasta again. Unthinkable.

She whispered Mamá's prayer. "Into Your hands, holy Father. Into Your hands."

In the entry to the dreaded lion's den, she paused, uncertain if she could take another step. Her whole body trembled.

"Good evening, gentlemen," she managed, releasing Jocasta's hand.

Iván stepped forward to pick up his daughter,

holding her little face to his, as if the day had been too long without her. "Good evening, Señorita. Good evening, my beloved daughter. How was your day?" His words included both, but his eyes were only on Jocasta.

Aurora allowed Elías to hold her chair and nodded to the unsmiling men around her. Raúl offered a sneer in return and he had no teasing words.

A swallow from her water tumbler enabled her to face Iván as he took his seat. He bowed his head and called on Justo to say grace. When he looked up, his gaze lingered on her for a moment. It was soft, reflecting no animosity.

Aurora sagged in her chair. It would be all right. There was no anger because she had not brought his daughter to breakfast. He was willing to put aside her hateful accusations. His expression was as inscrutable as ever, and she realized he worked at keeping his eyes from meeting hers.

He means to do his part to bridge the chasm as gently as possible.

His manner declared Aurora free to remain in the house on whatever footing she desired. He would allow her to set the pace between them. With that knowledge, she loved him more. The surge of emotion brought a tide of color to her face.

Her glance caught his before she lowered hers to concentrate on food she couldn't taste. Her hands were steady, but there was a ringing in her ears and she had to resort to inward prayer.

The men were uncharacteristically quiet during the meal. She risked a glance down the table. Justo met her eyes, but his face registered only customary disapproval. Raúl returned a bold, questioning gaze. He obviously sensed something he didn't like.

Elías smiled his sweet smile when Aurora turned to him with a question about the dogie calf he brought to the stable yard two days before.

"You must bring Jocasta in the morning to watch the little fellow, Señorita. He is at home with his foster mother now and thriving. A very grateful orphan. We need a name for him, Jocasta."

"I shall come in the morning with a name and a treat. We must get up early, Señorita Aurora, and breakfast with *Tío* Elías."

Smiling, Aurora agreed, aware that Iván studied her. She wanted to show her gratitude, but she could not meet that black gaze. Not yet.

Gritty eyes and a headache—what she needed was sleep. She excused herself as soon as possible.

It wasn't long before she drifted off, only to surface with a start. How long had she slept? The combination of deep sleep and sudden awakening cleared her head like a tonic, and left her mind remarkably sharp and focused.

She was not alone in the bedroom. *Holy Father, stay near, please.* Why had she left her door unlocked? Moonlight filtered through the shutters, illuminating her bed and beyond. Aurora peered through the veil of her lashes.

The outline of a man filled the door, silhouetted by light from the hallway's sconces. He was not tall enough for Iván. One of the other brothers? Or an intruder?

"Who is there?" Aurora kept her voice to a whisper. Jocasta's door was open.

He strode to the bed and leaned over her. "I must talk with you. Come with me downstairs."

Aurora swallowed her irritation. "Keep your voice down, Don Raúl." She smelled liquor on his breath. "You should not be here. Please leave."

"No. We must talk. You don't want a disturbance. Jocasta could wake. Or even Iván."

After a moment's indecision, she whispered, "Wait for me on the landing. I will join you after I am certain you have not awakened Jocasta."

Raúl left the door ajar behind him. Aurora snatched up her robe, found her slippers, and tiptoed into Jocasta's room. She almost laughed aloud. The little sleeper was a snail, legs curled beneath her, her backside in the air. Aurora pulled the coverlet higher and stood for a moment.

Second thoughts arose. She didn't fear Raúl, but she couldn't trust his judgment. He was a self-centered lothario, but even when he'd forced her to kiss him, he had turned it into a comic victory.

However, he was right. She couldn't avoid him without a scene.

Should she lock the door and risk the aftermath? Jocasta still had sleepless nights. She didn't need another one. And if Iván became involved, it could mean a deeper misunderstanding between them or a rift between the brothers.

"Holy Father," she whispered, "You are with me. Please give me the words for this man. He needs You in his life."

Raúl stood near her door, fully dressed. What

time was it? Surely far past midnight. He gripped her elbow with one hand, a candle in the other, and tried to steer her toward the stairs.

Aurora stood firm. "We can speak here, Don Rául. I will not leave Jocasta." She motioned toward a settee near the top of the stairs.

"No. We might awaken her. We'll go to the library. I have something to say that you must hear." Exasperating man. His voice was too loud. He meant to have his way.

She allowed him to tug her down the stairway and the length of the foyer, until they faced the office door. He opened it and pressed her inside. A key turned in the lock.

Watching her with an expression she could not read, Raúl placed it in his vest pocket. He stood, legs apart, hands at his sides. Something happened to the hairs on the back of her neck, but she squared her shoulders. Finish this now, before it got out of hand.

"What can be so urgent as to require a late-night consultation behind a locked door, Don Raúl?" Her voice held an edge.

He didn't answer, but strode across the room and picked up a candlestick from the mantel. Using the shortened candle in his hand to light it, he set the candlestick on the mantel, and tossed the stub into the embers. The spent log fell apart in a shower of sparks.

Shutters and draperies were drawn back. Moonlight and the light from garden torches poured through the stained glass, creating a weak shadow of its daytime rainbow. She stood stiffly near the door, her brow furrowed.

"Come nearer the fire, Aurora. You must be cold."

He tried to smile, but the result was not convincing. He was up to something and she suspected she wasn't going to like it. No choice but to go along with him for a while. Appeal to his reason.

He crossed the room and led her to the fireplace. The sense of foreboding strengthened. Why, oh why, had she come with this unpredictable man? Alone into a now-locked room?

Raúl lifted a crystal decanter from a nearby table and poured brandy into two short-stemmed glasses. She declined the one he offered, but he tossed down one and lifted the second in a salute, finishing it almost as quickly as the first.

Aurora adopted a challenging tone. "Don Raúl, please tell me what is on your mind before Jocasta awakens. It must be a matter of urgency for you to breach the sanctity of our rooms."

In two strides he had her in his arms. He whispered, "Aurora," and pulled her ever closer, despite her firm resistance.

She had to gain control of the situation, but her mind was a blank. Was this how it felt to wander into the powerful undertow of the sea? To watch the shoreline recede, knowing she did not have the strength to overcome its pull?

She pushed against Raúl's chest. He was so strong. "Please let me go. Now." He gave her a little space and she stared up at him.

His eyes narrowed. "I tire of the game you play with me."

"I have never sought to play with you, Don Raúl. You refuse to listen. Do not force something that does not exist for either of us."

His laugh was bitter. "Don't play the innocent, Aurora. You came into this house, a preposterously beautiful woman, with a voice lined in velvet. The tantalizer who remains just out of reach."

"Don Raúl—"

"I know some of what happened in this room last evening. I listened at the door. Iván found no joy, *¿verdad*?" For a moment his eyes were hard and heated. "You offer and then withhold."

"No. I never enticed him or you."

"The outcome will be different with me." His expression softened. "I am in love with you."

What was wrong with these men? She wanted to rush to the door and try to batter it open.

"What you feel is not love, Don Raúl. Love comes from sharing faith and common goals. Standing beside someone, facing hardships and obstacles together. Anything less is mere desire. My parents stressed—"

He shouted at her. "I am in love with you! It has cost me my pride and my relationship with my brothers, my entire outlook on life. I was carefree, taking life as it came, and women with it. Now I can think of no woman but you. I'm going crazy without you."

"Please listen, Don Raúl—"

He jerked her closer and hissed, "And you still address me as *Don* Raúl. Speak as if I'm a stranger. My name is Raúl Francisco, Aurora. I'm a flesh and blood man with deep feelings that are not to be trampled."

He was right. She'd failed to recognize his deeper emotional involvement, annoyed as she was by his continued attentions. Misjudged him, thinking he sought only to toy with her.

Friar Peralta counseled, "Always listen for the

heart beneath the words." Perhaps she could still reach him. Aurora abandoned her formal address and began to speak in the familiar.

"Forgive me if I've caused you pain. I have little experience with men, Raúl, so I apologize if I gave you reason to misunderstand me. I don't want to be the cause of dissension between you and your brothers, or heartbreak for you."

His mouth twisted. Was her new approach too late? "I don't want you to be unhappy. Please help me set things straight between us."

Raúl's eyes held a disturbing glitter, but he smiled. "How shall we set things straight, Aurora? What is your plan?"

"I care about you. You're witty and intelligent. I want us to be friends. I want the easy relationship with you that I enjoy with Elías. We laugh together and have good times. You and I can have that, too."

"Elías is a boy, Aurora. I am a man of strong passions and you have aroused them. Perhaps you didn't seek to draw me in, or perhaps you knew exactly how to weave your web around me. Who knows? Women are rarely honest with themselves."

"No, Raúl—"

"For a woman to be just out of reach is frustrating. You owe me an opportunity to make you love me as much as I love you."

He rested his arms on Aurora's shoulders and worked behind her head to undo her braid. She struggled to turn away and her hair fell about her face. Twisting his hands in it, he held her

"Only God could love you for yourself alone, Aurora, and not for this glorious mane." He buried his face in her neck, holding her close.

She suppressed the scream that echoed in her head. Pointless in this remote part of the house. Reason with him.

"You don't want to go against my will. Iván and your other brothers will not support you."

At the mention of Iván's name, Raúl uttered an expletive. "Iván does not control my life. I'll determine what takes place between us, not him." His hold became an embrace of iron and his hard mouth forced hers. He twisted his hand tighter in her hair.

Don't struggle—I must not fight him. He will lose control completely. Somehow Aurora found strength to remain motionless. At last, he raised his face from hers.

"You're hurting me." Aurora struggled to keep her voice steady. She had not believed capricious, sardonic Raúl capable of such anger and depth of feeling. He'd appeared a light-hearted flirt, but now he was in the grip of obsession. She bowed her head, closed her eyes, and prayed aloud so he could hear.

"Holy Father," her voice held a tremor, despite her best effort, "please forgive me for not recognizing the temptation I built in Raúl. Help him to forgive my unwillingness to talk with him and to place our problem before You…"

He shook her. "Enough! Stop your prayers! I don't want a holy resolution. I want one that will satisfy my need of you." He forced another kiss, but it was not as rough. "You're coming with me to the guest house. I've waited long enough. I love you, Aurora. I won't hurt you."

"No, Raúl. This has nothing to do with love. You cannot love me if you're willing to go against my will."

Raúl picked her up and headed toward the door, his mouth silencing her protests, but after a step or two, he stumbled and fell on top of her. Breath whooshed from her lungs and blackness closed in.

Fifteen

When Aurora opened her eyes she was on a couch, the same one chosen by Iván, near the fireplace. Her chest ached and her head throbbed. She felt bruised and weary.

Raúl knelt beside her, chafing her wrists and calling her name. "Aurora! Wake up. Tell me you're all right. Say I haven't hurt you."

She wanted to cry. When would this frightening escapade end? "Please help me sit up. I can't breathe."

Raúl pulled her up and into his arms, kissing the top of her head. "*Preciosa,*" he moaned. "I acted insanely. I never meant to hurt you. Say I haven't ruined everything between us." He searched her face. "But nothing has changed. We must finish what we started."

What next?

"I said the wrong things to you." His expression was uncertain, his eyes wild.

"Raul, it's late. We can finish this tomorrow. I must go to Jocasta."

"No, it must be said." His voice became a hoarse

whisper. "If it's marriage you want, Aurora, I will marry you. I have never said that to any woman, but I must have you."

She stared at him. A sour and bitter taste filled her mouth. He'd hurt her and frightened her, and now he proposed *marriage*? She rubbed at her aching arms, striving for control. Anger would not serve her.

Fray Peralta thought she might be able to influence the spiritual lives of the men, as unlikely as that seemed to her. These minutes mattered to God. Raúl should not be fixating on her. His soul was at stake. But she was at a loss. All she cared about was getting away.

He said, "Iván cannot marry you, but I can, and I will."

Cannot marry me? Iván said the same.

"I have plans, Aurora. We can share a fine life together. Make a true empire of Rancho de Montaraz. Or we can live anywhere in the world. We're not bound to this family or to this ranch. Iván will have to recognize your legitimate claim."

She snapped at him. "What are you talking about? What claim could I possibly have here?"

"You can legitimately claim the name de Montaraz—the only one in this house who can. We brothers are adopted to the name, but you are the daughter of León de Montaraz. His only blood child. Iván should have told you before now."

She shook her head. "Ridiculous. I don't believe you. You're being spiteful because I wouldn't give in to you. Open the door, Raúl. I want to leave. You can't keep me prisoner."

"I'm speaking the truth, Aurora. Why would I invent such a lie?"

It could not be true, but something in his manner gave her pause. Why would he invent such a story? She sought her crucifix. "Are you saying León de Montaraz had a love child with some woman? That he gave me to my mother and father?"

"You are her daughter, Aurora. You share your mother's blood and his."

Blood rushed from her face. *Despicable! Mother would never!* Aurora's hand rose to slap the face of the man who would disgrace her mother's memory, but Raúl caught it as easily as he had before.

"No, no, little spirited one. Listen to me."

"Let me go. You are disgusting."

"Antonio Rivera was not your physical father. The proof is in a letter my father left before his death. The padres at the mission know the true story."

She stopped her struggles. Fray Peralta knew when he asked her to come?

"And you look amazingly like León de Montaraz. You have his eyes, his mouth and smile. Even his widow's peak. That first night when you had your hair up, I thought I was looking at a female incarnation of my father."

This cannot be true.

"In a letter of testament, Father asked Iván to bring you into the family. He wished you to share his name and fortune. A generous gesture—most illegitimates are never recognized among families of wealth." Raúl seemed relaxed now that he had said his piece. He had the look of a man who spoke truth.

Aurora struggled for breath. Her whole body shook. "I will have to see this purported letter before I believe you."

"Easily arranged. Think, *querida,*" Raúl crooned, "together we can make of this ranch the empire my father intended. Iván is satisfied with too little. We can do great things. Anything. We can help the poor, so dear to your heart."

Her head spun. She moaned. *My mother and the father of these men?* How was she to understand all this in the light of God's purpose?

I'm going to faint. Her knees buckled and Raúl steadied her in his arms. Through a haze she heard a key rattle in the lock and watched Iván stalk across the office, shirt half-open and untucked. Aurora stared at him. He was no apparition. His black eyes snapped fire and his face was stiff.

"What is this, Aurora? An assignation in my office while your charge is left alone and frightened in her bed? Jocasta called for you. I heard her from the other side of the house. You could have heard her here, had you not been involved in other matters." His mouth twisted. "She is with Luisa, and you are in Raúl's embrace."

Iván took hold of her arm and jerked her toward him, glaring at his brother. Raúl bristled and stepped forward.

Anger cleared the fog from Aurora's brain. What right had Iván to reproach her? She was created for God's purposes, not as a pawn of these men. Wresting her arm from Iván's grip, she whirled to meet his accusing eyes.

"Ask your brother how I came to be here, Don Iván, and what transpired between us. You missed the opening scene. Raúl has completed his fervent blandishments and reached the crux of the matter: a proposal of marriage to the only blood child of Don León de Montaraz."

Iván's eyes widened. His face went slack. He whispered, "Aurora."

Silence lay like a blanket. No one moved for what seemed like minutes. Then Iván shot Raúl an angry glare. "Aurora, I planned to tell you—"

"Let's go, Aurora. You don't have to listen to this." Raúl reached for her, but Iván blocked him with an outstretched arm.

"Raúl finds the idea of marriage appealing on several levels. He wants me in his bed enough to marry me, he said. And then there is the matter of an increased inheritance." She threw out her hands and stepped back. "I don't want to hear from either of you." Her voice shook. "At last, I understand the hostility I encountered when I entered the domain of León de Montaraz. His sons did not want to share their fortune or their elevated status with the daughter of a *vaquero* and a teacher of Indian children."

Iván shook his head. "Aurora, you don't—"

"I must be a very unfitting candidate for such prominence, or you would have offered to marry me long ago, Don Iván, to cement your own position to a larger claim. What is it you see lacking in me that Raúl does not?"

Neither man moved or spoke. They stared at her, their loss for words written on their faces.

Aurora murmured, "You sicken me. Your father asked you to take compassion on a daughter he was not willing to acknowledge or care for in his lifetime. One who must have lain heavy on his conscience at the end, if what Raúl says has any truth. Things look different to men just before they go to their Maker."

The men eyed one another uneasily.

"This is your work, Iván. You silenced Fray Peralta through his vows of confidentiality because you decided to allow your sister to live as a servant in your house. A clever way to prevent any leak of the unwelcome story." Aurora shivered in the light robe. She closed her eyes, a hand to her mouth. How could any man be so perfidious?

It was hard to think of Iván in this vein. She'd believed in his integrity until this moment. Believed he had a legitimate reason for not marrying her.

"You don't understand, Aurora." Iván's face showed his anguish. His hand lay on her arm.

She removed it. "I believe I do. Work this out with the other two. Then, my brothers of distinction, after you find a solution to your problem of an unwanted sister, present it to me. I can decide how to react. Fray Peralta will advise me."

Aurora's head throbbed. Her words became listless. "There was no risk. You could have told me the truth at the start. I want no part of the de Montaraz name or fortune." A sob escaped.

Raúl said, "Aurora, you're confused. Let me—"

"My true father was compassionate and honorable, accepting the child of another man, if you are to be believed. He loved and nurtured that child to his last breath. Yours apparently was not his equal."

Iván looked about to explode, but neither he nor Raúl offered a word in their defense. Would she listen if they did? Her self-control was in shreds. She wanted only to get away.

"As you say, Don Iván, Jocasta needs me." She

stalked through the door and came face to face with Justo and Elías. They stood half-clothed.

Aurora took a candlestick from Elías' hand and climbed the stairs to the child who owned her heart. Free reign to her anger and spiteful words had failed to offer comfort. She needed to hold Jocasta in her arms.

The muddle Iván had made must not harm her relationship with Jocasta. But she must acknowledge the precious child belonged to him. What would he do?

"Your plan has not worked, Iván. Bring her into the house, you said. Check out her worthiness to bear the name of de Montaraz." Raúl's hands balled into fists.

"What were you doing with her? She didn't look happy about it," Iván growled. "And you revealed what was not yours to tell. I planned to find a way to disclose the facts soon. Perhaps bring Fray Peralta here. You are the one who ruined everything with your lack of control."

Raúl laughed. His voice was bitter. "I've never had control of anything. You're just like Father. You alone make the decisions for all of us. It's time things changed, and I mean to see they do. I mean to marry Aurora, and you cannot stop me."

He turned his back on Iván and strolled toward the door, then paused and looked from his waiting brothers to the rigid figure staring into the dying fire.

"I should not be surprised if my other brothers join in the rebellion. Good night, Iván. Sleep well."

Sixteen

Luisa put her finger to her lips as Aurora tiptoed into the room. She took the chair beside Jocasta's bed and Luisa tried to ease away, but the little girl opened her eyes.

"Don't go, Luisa. Stay with me."

Aurora bent over her and said, "I'm here."

"Where were you, Señorita Aurora?" She sobbed and her arms reached out. "I had a bad dream and you did not come when I screamed. Papá came and called for Luisa. Why did you leave me?"

Aurora sat and cradled her. "I wasn't far away, *preciosa.* But remember this. You're in the care of two fathers. Your Heavenly One and your earthly one." She wiped a tear from a glistening cheek. "You need never be afraid."

Jocasta put her arms around Aurora's neck. "Please do not ever leave me again!"

"I hope we never have to part, but life has its turns. If I ever have to be away from you, I'll still be near you in my heart and in my prayers." She smiled.

"I need you here with me."

"Would you like to spend the rest of the night in my big bed? We can snuggle and laugh if we don't make too much noise. Others will be trying to sleep, but we can stay awake as long as we wish. We'll open the shutters to let in the moonlight, tell stories, and sleep as late as we want."

Jocasta giggled at the thought of such delights. "Luisa can bring breakfast. We can eat and even study there."

Aurora scooped her up and laughed. "You'll tire of bed before school time, sweet one, but we can persuade Luisa to bring our breakfast. We must try not to get too many crumbs on the linens, or I may have a wee mouse for my bed partner tomorrow night."

Jocasta laughed most of the way to Aurora's bed. "Your room looks like it is under water."

Moonlight filtering between the shutters' slats wavered in a watery glow. Aurora opened the shutters wide and tucked Jocasta beneath the downy comforter. After an hour filled with whispers and subdued giggles, she sang Jocasta to sleep with an old Spanish lullaby of Mamá's.

In a tormenting first hour after Jocasta drifted off, Aurora's mind seethed with questions. How could her mother breach her faith and the trust of a woman in her care? Such a selfish act.

It made no sense. Anna Rivera had lived in devotion to her God, to her husband and daughters, and to the children she taught. Mamá's greatest joy had been serving others.

Couldn't Fray Peralta have prepared her somehow before she came among the brothers? He was bound by his vows, but there was something more. Somehow Fray Peralta saw God's purpose in her coming to the ranch. A purpose she could not understand. She sighed a long surrender.

She must continue to trust. God had a reason for her to be among these aggravating, perplexing, and sometimes frightening men, but how could He use her now? Two of them were at one another's throats, and a third despised her. Had she already failed?

There would be no sleep. She was the product of stolen love. Her beloved mother had entered a liaison with another woman's husband. But her spirit decided to wait for God to give understanding. With the child in her arms and a prayer in her troubled soul, she slept.

Breakfast was served in bed to two sleepy beauties, amid crumbs and laughter. Aurora pretended to see a mouse feasting, and Jocasta promptly gave the imaginary intruder a name. He was to be called "*Sonriendo*" because he was a mouse who liked to smile.

"And why does he smile?" Aurora asked.

"Because his whiskers tickle." Jocasta dissolved into giggles.

True to Aurora's prediction, the busybody didn't want to linger in bed, so the two worked at a few lessons and then headed to the swimming cove on Corazón. Aurora used a cross saddle Elías had outgrown because it was easier to manage Jocasta in her lap. Iván could object later.

It was an unseasonably warm day. The two waded in the shallows and then had lunch and a nap in warm blankets on sweet, cool grass, undisturbed by the de Montaraz men. None of them would want to face her before they had to.

She and Jocasta would appear at the dinner table. Aurora would not bend before the anger of Iván, the scorn of Justo, or Raúl's demands. She belonged among them for a reason known only to God. So why the quiver in her stomach?

That evening Aurora dressed with particular care. She wished she still had one of her old dresses. She'd have gone in rags. She didn't want to wear a dress bought by de Montaraz riches, but hers were gone. She had given them to María and Luisa when Iván directed Maria to make six new ones.

She chose instead the finest dress she owned, a russet Byzantine silk which María said picked up colors in her hair and flattered her skin. It might give her confidence and be a sign to the brothers that she would not wilt under pressure. She suggested Jocasta also wear one of her best, knowing she needed little urging.

Aurora's dress was a departure from the Empire waists she customarily wore. She had worn it only once, at a dress-up tea she and Jocasta shared. In her bold state of mind, it became the correct choice for the evening.

The silk was fashioned with a fitted bodice that exposed a slight décolletage. Her shoulders arose pale and taut above abbreviated sleeves that left her smooth arms unclad. The dress begged for ornate jewelry, but only her mother's silver cross adorned her neck.

She brushed Jocasta's hair and her own until both wore shining halos of contrasting glory. Aurora's glowed with golden highlights, embellished only with the combs her father carved. Jocasta's crackled with life, its curls gleaming in fiery radiance as Aurora tucked a pink shell rose beneath a small comb on either side of Jocasta's head.

The two descended the stairs and entered the dining room. Aurora looked squarely at each of the men standing around the table.

"Good evening." Her voice sounded huskier than usual, but she stood straight. She was surprised she could speak at all past the ache in her throat. *Into your hands, Holy Father.*

Jocasta ran to her father's open arms. Elías pulled out Aurora's chair. She spread her napkin with icy fingers, and took a sip of water. Hard to swallow. How could she possibly get through this meal?

She raised her head to four pairs of eyes riveted on her. She looked from one to the other and the gazes fell away. All except Iván's. His expression once more belonged on a statue or a coin.

Justo offered prayer. Aurora pushed the food around her plate, taking a few small bites. Jocasta proved to be a life-saver with her bright chatter, which needed little response.

Once Aurora caught Raúl's searching gaze, and another time Justo's, but neither spoke. Elías shifted beside her and she saw his hand tremble on his goblet.

The meal blessedly ended earlier than usual. Luisa came for Jocasta, and Aurora excused herself to accompany them, but Iván's hand was on her arm.

"Señorita Aurora, will you remain? My brothers and I have things to say if you are willing to hear us. We can talk in the library."

She stared at him, unable to speak. After a pause, she nodded, her stomach in a knot. Why she was willing to subject herself to more of the brothers?

Iván pulled out her chair and waited for her to cross the foyer ahead of him. In the library, armchairs had been arranged in a loose circle near the fire. Tables alternated between, each holding glasses of water. Two five-armed candelabras offered a comforting glow.

Iván took a seat directly across from the chair she chose, with Justo and Elías flanking her, looking ill-at-ease. She sympathized with their discomfiture, all the while trying to think of an excuse to escape. Raúl glared at his brothers and took the remaining chair.

Iván stared at the floor. His extraordinary stillness rendered time fluid and erratic. Was she in a trance? She was unsure whether seconds or minutes passed before his black gaze speared hers.

She caught a breath. Had she imagined the fire she'd once seen in those eyes? She could read nothing in them now.

"Each of us has something to say, Señorita Aurora. Elías has asked permission to speak first. We do not expect you to respond, but please hear us out." He once again wore the mantle of command.

Elías stood. "Señorita Aurora—" His voice sounded high. He flushed and cleared his throat. "I wish to ask your forgiveness." He'd chosen formal Spanish, as had Iván.

"I was a timid friend," Elías continued. "I could have done more to make you comfortable, and I was as guilty as any of withholding truth from you. If you will consent to forgive me, I will be a much happier man." He blinked and raked his hand through his hair, a familiar gesture. His esteem for Iván bordered on worship.

"You're forgiven, Elías. You've been a better

friend than you know. I've enjoyed many good times with you and Jocasta at the cove." She spoke as she usually did to him, in the familiar. When she smiled, he sagged into his chair. Tears shone in his eyes.

Justo stood ramrod straight, his hands clasped behind his back, looking directly ahead. He mumbled, "I, too, regret my actions, Señorita Rivera. My guilt is greater than Elías'. I never gave you a chance."

"We cannot hear you," said Iván.

Justo frowned at him, and drawing an audible breath, he stood taller. "I was angered by what I perceived as the betrayal of my mother by yours. Iván has pointed out to me, on more than one occasion, that I blamed you for circumstances of which I had no understanding and you had no control. I have not acted either fairly or honorably, and I regret it."

A sheen of perspiration dewed his brow, and a lump rose in Aurora's throat.

How trying for this proud man.

He slogged on, his gaze on the ceiling. "I think my true anger is against our father. Our mother was a good woman and if she learned of his infidelity, she suffered. She must have forgiven him, because they lived together for years and adopted sons."

He looked at his brothers. "We cannot place the blame solely on your mother. Father had a choice and it was he who was bound by vows before God to a wife." He sounded sincere, not merely mouthing words Iván had forced on him.

"Mamá was not blameless," Aurora whispered.

Justo sighed a frustrated sound. "I am not worthy of your forgiveness, but I do want you to understand I regret my bitter persecution. You did not deserve it."

His gaze finally held Aurora's. It was the first time he'd looked at her without censure.

She answered in the familiar. "I forgive you, Justo, as I'm forgiven by our God. You must understand forgiveness, being a devout man. Every one of us in this circle is a capable of great cruelty to others. If we can't forgive each other, there's no hope."

"*Gracias,* Señorita." He sat down and reached for a glass of water, swallowing audibly in the silence.

Raúl leaned forward in his chair and stared at her, his handsome face aged beyond its boyishness of months ago. He alone of the brothers addressed her in the familiar.

"I don't know what to say, Aurora, but I refuse to play the hypocrite. My feelings haven't changed. I say again before my brothers that I'm in love with you, but not a single one of them is convinced my love is good enough for you. You'll have to decide."

Gone was the confident, teasing *caballero* of the past. The angry man of the evening before had vanished with the passionate, reckless one. His cheeks were flushed and his mouth drooped.

Her heart constricted. What had she done to him? Aurora waited, convinced he had more to say.

Raúl drew a hand over his mouth and down his chin. "I'm sorry I tormented you in our early acquaintance, Aurora, and I wish I'd approached you differently last night. I have never before tried to force a woman."

He glared at Iván, who scowled in return.

"But I will not retract my offer to marry you. I've never known a woman like you. I love you for more reasons that I could enumerate last night." He stared at her. Waiting for another cutting word? She'd been so angry last night. So frightened and hateful.

"Thank you, Raúl, for your honesty. I won't try to deny you've caused me miserable moments, but I always wanted your regard."

His mouth turned downward.

"I chose to ignore you—or tried to. You can be a difficult man to ignore." He returned her smile with a weak one.

"I promise before your brothers to learn more of the real you. I've always felt that under that cavalier attitude lives another man. One I hope will give me a chance as friend."

Raúl shook his head. "Probably more than I deserve, Aurora, but I want more than friendship. I know I can satisfy you with my devotion."

She didn't answer. What he felt for her was not love as Papá had for Mamá. Perhaps he wanted to succeed with her where he imagined Iván had failed.

Every eye turned to Iván. He continued to stare at the floor as the silence lengthened. What would he have to say?

Seventeen

Iván stood without hesitation. "A part of what I have to say is for everyone in this group, and some is for you alone, Aurora, if you will consent to remain after the others leave."

Not alone with him. How could she bear it?

"When we read Father's letter asking us to receive you as a sister, I said we should wait. Become better acquainted with your character."

Raúl nodded, his face dark and accusing. Justo stared at his hands folded in his lap. Only Elías' expression showed sympathy.

"Father drummed into me that I was to preserve the unity of the family after he was gone. I decided you could become a divisive factor."

"I sensed your mistrust, Don Iván."

"We never meant to defraud you of your inheritance. We agreed at the outset you would get your share, whether or not you were asked to remain. If we agreed your performance warranted, we would offer you the proud name of de Montaraz."

I never wanted it. Papá's is far more honorable.

"My arrogance disgusts me." His voice took on an edge. "I was wrong. Fray Peralta warned me from the beginning that truth was the way. The time to tell you never came. My cowardice, no doubt. And other feelings."

Other feelings, indeed.

Elías coughed and reached for his glass. The brothers stared at Iván. The others seemed as surprised as she at his lengthy explanation.

Iván put a hand to his forehead, covering his eyes. "There is nothing I could ever do to earn your forgiveness, Aurora, but I want you to know I bitterly regret my ill-conceived plan and other actions. You are a much finer person than any of us."

None of his brothers disagreed. They appeared unable to speak.

Aurora's voice shook. "Iván, forgiveness is not an option for one who follows God. It's a command, as much for my benefit as yours." She looked at the other faces and gained strength. "Before your brothers, I forgive you. I hope we can go forward in greater understanding."

Iván's eyes widened and his expression brightened. The others studied the floor as if searching for inspiration. It was time.

"It's my turn, brothers." The silence felt heavy with uncertainty. "I confess when I first came I saw you as proud, aristocratic men, and labeled you uncaring."

Justo looked taken aback, and the others wary.

"Friar Peralta warned me of your united front. I felt the outsider and blamed you, but as I lived among you, I began to recognize your regard for each other and your love for Jocasta. I wanted you to accept me, but I must have looked a hopeless prig. Raúl once said he was surprised to find me swimming. As if I should have found the sport beneath me."

He nodded. What else did he remember?

"My mother was reared in gentility, but she never tried to hold me back from a natural life, just as you encourage Jocasta."

"Señorita Aurora—" Elias began.

"Wait, *hermano*. Let her finish," Iván ordered.

"I had a secure childhood, *caballeros*, but not a privileged one. I played in the dirt with native children." Aurora smiled, remembering.

"We painted our faces and bodies in the way of wild tribesmen and fashioned tule skirts. Fished and cooked our catch over campfires. Tried out some of the soldiers' profanity and played naughty tricks on the padres. The confessional became a familiar haunt. We once stole a cigar from the *comandante* of the presidio. Smoked it and became properly sick."

The brothers looked at each other and grinned. They could relate.

"My father was a *vaquero*. He would have recognized much of himself in you; and I should have, but I chose to think of you as sons of privilege, who did not think in terms of love and loyalty. But I've discovered that you do. All of you."

Iván glanced toward Raúl, who returned a glare.

"You're honest, hard-working men. You send provisions to the mission. The houses you provide are far superior to those on other ranches. You care for the sick and all who come your way. You follow God's commands."

The brothers stared at her.

Yes, brothers, you do the work of God, whether or not you think in those terms.

"And I've learned you were once orphans like me. We have more in common than I knew. Most of all, we have in common a profound love for Jocasta and a desire to help her grow into a fine woman."

Aurora thought for several moments. None of the men moved or made a sound.

"It feels good to sit in your midst and to hear admissions from you that must be very difficult. I was prepared for further estrangement and hostility. You humble me. I forgive you all, my brothers, and I ask you to forgive me in return."

The men looked at Aurora as if seeing her for the first time.

"God is removing scales of mistrust and judgment from our eyes, brothers, and offering us new relationships."

Elías smiled at her and Justo nodded.

Iván rose and said, "I believe I speak for my brothers as well as myself when I say we do not deserve your grace. Brothers, I ask you to leave me with our sister. I need to talk to her in private."

Only Raúl showed reluctance. He started to speak, but when Iván's expression darkened he appeared to think again, instead following the others out of the room.

Aurora suppressed an urge to call out to him. She felt small in her chair—vulnerable, and unprepared as Iván towered over her.

Iván settled his lengthy frame after he turned Justo's vacated chair to face Aurora. Their knees almost touched. For a moment she considered jumping up and running for the door. She stared at Iván, drained and listless. It had all been said.

"Whenever I'm alone with you, Aurora, I seem to choose the wrong words, but I want to tell you all of the truth. Are you willing to listen?" Sincerity flooded from him.

She must look as hesitant as she felt. Fresh in her mind were the thrill of his arms, his kisses. The pain when he destroyed her hope. There could be no marriage. Even Raúl said it. What else could be said?

"To what end, Iván? I'm not certain I want to know. I did that evening, but God has given me grace to deal with the knowledge that you'll never marry me. To know the reason will demand a new surrender and the end result will be the same."

"The decision is yours, Aurora. I don't want to add to the pain I have already caused."

Iván posed danger to her carefully-crafted peace of mind. How much greater the peril if she learned the shape of his heart?

He picked up a candlestick and held it near his face. "Look at me, Aurora."

"Eyes are windows into our souls," Mamá once told her. "They tell others what we feel and they invite response."

Iván's had been closed doors that evening in the library. All she'd seen in those black mirrors had been a reflection of her anguish. Now he waited for her permission to reopen the wound.

She couldn't help herself. Once more she stared into the eyes of Iván de Montaraz—all the way into his soul. The sensation was at first frightening, then hypnotic. This man, who had guarded his thoughts so jealously, now offered access to his deepest feelings.

"Iván," she moaned. "You love me. You want what's best for me. Why are you not right for me if you feel this genuine caring? Tell me. I want to know why we cannot marry."

The words burst from him. "She lives, Aurora! The mother of Jocasta lives. My lie to you and to the world is that she is dead. My brothers know the truth. A few others on this hacienda, and the friars. But to Jocasta and the rest of the world she is dead."

Aurora gasped. "Why in the world, Iván? How can you condone such deceit?"

He put his fist to his mouth, the gesture of a desolate man. She clasped her hands together to keep them from holding his face and kissing away his pain. He had a wife.

Iván bowed his head. She had to strain to hear the words he murmured. "Lucera tried to kill Jocasta."

Had she heard correctly?

His strong chin trembled for a heart-breaking moment. "She threw her infant daughter down the stairs, hoping she would die. Jocasta was grievously injured, but she recovered. Everything but her eyesight. It is irreparably harmed."

"Why, Iván? Why would she want to destroy her own perfect child? I cannot understand."

"My wife is insane, Aurora. She hates her own child. Lucera would destroy Jocasta tonight if she could reach her. Often she believes she has already killed her. The woman has no concept of reality."

Aurora fought her revulsion. Iván needed to confess, but was she strong enough to bear it?

"Soon after Mother's death, Father offered me his choice for a wife and I did not question it. Lucera and I met only a few times and never alone. When she reached her majority we married. Father later learned she was mentally unstable."

Arranged marriages were not always made in heaven. Aurora thought of Mamá's weak-willed suitor, Pedro, who abandoned her when he learned her fortune was gone.

"The birth of Jocasta pushed her into insanity. A profound, dark depression. Lucera lives only to hate—her child, her existence, and me. She would destroy herself if she were not watched at all times."

Warmth flooded Aurora. God had preserved Jocasta's life. Iván's daughter was his solace—made his pain bearable.

Tears stood in his eyes. "I've consulted doctors. None can restore her. Lucera lives in isolation on this ranch because it's the only way to assure her protection and the safety of our daughter. I've tried, Aurora. I have tried." He rubbed the back of his neck and took a deep breath.

Aurora's mind raced, but she found no words of comfort. No wisdom for him. The silence lengthened.

Iván knelt and took her hands. He rubbed his long thumbs across her knuckles and raised his eyes. "I fell in love with you, knowing I had no right. I chose to love you anyway, seeing so much to love."

She couldn't deny him. She had to find strength to hear whatever he needed to say. Fray Peralta said Iván did not consult the friars. The weight of her new role made her chest ache. She could foresee other times as she listened, suffering with him. But she could turn to prayer. Iván didn't know God's comfort.

"I cannot fix on the hour or the circumstance when it began, Aurora, this love for you. I was in the midst of it before I recognized what had happened."

Her eyelids stung, but she must be strong. Tears would burden him further.

"I love your kindness, your fidelity to your faith, your courage, and your unwavering devotion to my daughter. My little daughter who tried so hard to drive you away. I love the way you touch her life—all of life—and make it bloom."

How much more could she bear?

He stared up at her. "And I love you for you, although I can't explain exactly what I mean. But I have no right to love you as a man loves a woman."

Iván's fists clenched and opened. "I vowed I would never do to you what my father did to your mother, yet I allowed myself to try. I lost control, Aurora! I lost control!"

The ultimate sin for Iván. How he must berate himself. And she had heaped on more scorn.

He whispered. "I understand Father as Justo never will. A man with faults and graces, Aurora, as men are." He cleared his throat. "I believe he loved both women, but he failed them in the same manner I did. I ruined a trusting relationship you worked hard to build because I want what I cannot have. Knowing your faith makes divorce impossible, I still want you with me forever."

Aurora did not respond. She couldn't say what was in her heart. She must conceal her own truth.

Iván arose, walked to the end of the room, and stared out into the night. She waited without moving.

He returned and rested his elbows on the back of his chair, a safeguard between them.

"I first thought Father forced the marriage between your mother and Antonio, but Fray Peralta said she chose the higher road."

He sat again and stared at her hands. She realized she was flexing them in her lap, fingertips together, like a beating heart. She stopped the movement and hung her head.

Aurora was horrified to hear herself say, "You're not alone, Iván. Only God's purpose within me, directing me to stay for Jocasta, enabled me to face this day without you." What was she doing?

His gaze met hers in such intensity that she faltered. *Should I go on? It's true.*

"I couldn't understand how Mamá could make a decision that hurt others so profoundly, until I heard your story. She gave León what she believed he needed and took what she wanted. Right now I wish I had her courage or her weakness, whatever the case. I want to throw myself into your arms—"

Iván leaped to his feet and turned away. "No, Aurora! Do not tempt me. You're not your mother and I'm not my father. I cannot let you live in disobedience to your beliefs."

She wept then, her hands over her face. He didn't try to comfort her. Finally he took her hands and pulled her up. They walked toward the door.

"Your forgiveness for my brothers and me offers me hope, Aurora. Perhaps God can help me to become a better man."

"Yes, Iván! God will help us both."

"It has to be enough to love you and not try to

satisfy selfish longings. I want to learn to love the way you've learned—from God."

He tipped up her chin. "Can you trust me? Will you allow me to hold you the way I should have the first time, Aurora? I should have hugged you in celebration and let you go. Now I want only to comfort you, *querida*."

Aurora melted against him. His strong heart drummed beneath her ear. Her sobs eased as he stroked her hair.

He murmured. "I'll learn to want only what is good for you. If it's Raúl, then I must let you go. If you choose him, I must learn to love you as a sister."

Fresh sobs wracked her body. "Never Raúl! I will love only you until the day I die." She dashed away her tears. "But you're right. We cannot steal our happiness from a confused woman. I want you to allow me to love you, as well. We'll trust one another and God."

The sadness in Iván's eyes aged him, but a new expression shone on his face. "Beloved, sleep tonight in the knowledge that I seek to place myself in God's hands. I want to learn to trust Him for strength to love you and Jocasta—and yes, my wife—in the way He intends. There has to be a way, Aurora."

"My father said when one door closes, God opens another, and we should not look at the closed one so long that we miss the new opening."

But how will that work out for Iván and me?

Eighteen

The healing between her and three of the brothers heartened Aurora. But she ached with Raúl's rejection.

He'd stopped coming to meals and moved into the guest house. The few times she saw him, he'd been drinking. Iván didn't want to talk about him, but Aurora couldn't give up on him. She felt a responsibility since he fancied himself in love with her.

"Someone needs to reach out to him," she said.

Iván's expression turned grim. "If I can find the strength to deal with my disappointment, so can Raúl. He's a man, Aurora. He wouldn't welcome my meddling."

Men could be so frustrating, protecting their manly images. But Iván's words were a caution. Raúl would not welcome her advice, either. Men resisted emotion. Iván sometimes seemed embarrassed when he spoke of his own lengthy confession. But there must be a way to reach Raúl.

Aurora had Jocasta, her joy and refuge from

problems. She spent as much time with the little girl as possible. This late afternoon, the two of them and Elías were throwing a ball in the courtyard for Jocasta's new puppy. The ball rolled toward the house and Aurora searched the flower bed beneath the office window on hands and knees. She tossed it back to Elías and froze. From the open side window heated voices poured out.

Raúl said, "Why should I believe you want what's best for me? You didn't care when Father was alive. You never tried to include me in what the two of you shared." His words were slurred.

"Not true. I've always tried to do what's best for my brothers."

"You decide what's best? We're no longer boys. Perhaps it's time for the brothers to go separate ways. You have no right to tell another grown man what he can or cannot do."

I don't want to hear this. But she couldn't leave. Any movement might draw their attention.

"And you pursue the woman I want, even though you cannot marry her. You're just like Father. A wealthy, aristocratic wife was not enough for either of you; you also want a beautiful lover. You try to control everyone on this ranch but don't care about anyone but yourself. Suddenly you want what's good for me?"

Aurora gasped. *No, Raúl. You're wrong!*

Iván's deep voice remained calm, but his words were clipped. Aurora imagined the flat stare, impassive face and long, grim mouth.

"I make no claims on Aurora. She's free to choose you, and I think you know that. I've told her of my marriage and she agrees I must honor my vows. We are not lovers."

His voice softened. "We're not going to allow you to become a worthless drunk, Raúl. Your brothers and I have decided you'll move back into the main house. If we need to, one of us will be with you at all times. We care about you."

"So you say." Raul's laugh was derisive.

"We're in agreement. Either move your things back in, or we'll do it for you. Come to meals with us, or we'll come to get you."

"Why should I listen to you?"

"Because you must follow the law of family."

Aurora heard him rise and move away from the desk. She stole away from the window.

Raúl was in his customary place at dinner. He sat in silence. When he caught Aurora's gaze, he raised one sardonic eyebrow. Justo's face flushed and he tried to engage Raúl in conversation. He ignored Justo, took two bites of his steak, and said, "My glass is empty." When Jorge finished pouring the wine, Raúl took the bottle.

Justo and Elías watched with troubled eyes as he drained it, sans glass. Jocasta cast puzzled glances at her sullen uncle.

Iván's drumming fingers betrayed his reaction, but they stopped when he noticed Aurora watching.

When her father pulled Jocasta's chair back, she made her way down the table and stood beside Raúl. She pulled his face down until their noses almost touched.

"*Tío*, you look sad. Why have you been away so often? I'll make an especially beautiful dried arrangement for you tomorrow. Señorita Aurora has taught me that even in winter plants have beauty. I'll put them in your room to remind you how much I love you and how much God loves you."

Raúl reached out and lifted her into his lap. Nuzzling her sweet face, he said, "I'm not sad, *preciosa,* but I do want those flowers."

He chucked her under the chin. "Study hard. You'll grow up to be the most beautiful and intelligent woman in two *Californias*." He kissed her and left the table.

Aurora looked toward Iván. Surely he'd follow and try again to restore the relationship. Iván met her gaze and shrugged, then stood to pull out her chair. She wanted to cry.

"I need some time alone," Aurora said the next day. Iván nodded and Jocasta danced away, tugging on his hand, ready for a new adventure with her Papá. They were on their way to the port, but Aurora headed for the *corrales* and asked the stable boy to saddle Corazón. She'd spent a restless night, thinking of Raúl. If Iván would not reach out, she must try; but how?

She turned the mare toward the orchard, dug in her heels, and they were off. They flashed past the trees, riding toward the river. The feel of her hair whipping about and the powerful grace of the animal beneath her shut out her worries.

Occasional clouds and patches of fog jockeyed with the sun in an azure sky. In the distance they gathered to shroud tops of blue-violet peaks. The air was filled with moisture and the elusive hints of approaching winter. Wearing only a light jacket, Aurora soaked up warming rays of the sun. After several minutes she pulled back on the reins and slowed to a trot, allowing the mare to catch her breath.

"The sun feels good. I needed this. Just you, Corazón, and the Holy Father. You won't mind hearing my troubles, will you? I need to speak them. Sometimes hearing my words clarifies my thinking."

The mare looked over her shoulder and snorted. "All right. I brought a treat, but don't think of it as a bribe." Aurora pulled a carrot from inside her jacket and Corazón drew back her lips. She accepted her treat and munched contentedly.

"My heart aches for Iván, but just as much for Raúl. He holds onto his obsession about me." She sighed. "All of us want what we should not have. I want Iván and he wants me, but we trust God and one another. Raúl struggles alone."

Aurora changed Corazón's direction and, after a few minutes, topped the rise overlooking the cove. Below her, standing near the large rock at the mouth of the cove, stood Raúl, his back to her. His horse grazed nearby. Her first instinct was to turn away, but she held to her resolve.

Tension characterized every line of his body. She could hear his voice, but no one else was in sight. Aurora was reminded of Iván the evening he stood with his hand on the mantel and all that followed. And then Raúl's rough assault.

She was alone.

But God loved this man. Raúl was important to Him, and so he must be to her. She couldn't just stand aside and watch him slide into debauchery.

Before she could rethink her decision, Aurora guided Corazón down the hill through the rim of sheltering willows. Raúl's words remained indistinguishable. He didn't turn until she was close behind him. When she saw his expression she halted. Raúl took several steps toward her. His face showed the same torment of the night when he declared his intent to take her.

"Raúl," Aurora began, but he growled, "Don't leave that horse. What are you doing here?"

"I came to ask you the same, Raúl. We've had no real opportunity to talk since that night in the library when things went badly. I know your brothers are very concerned. Jocasta asks me about *Tío* Raúl. Will you talk to me for a few minutes?" She remained in the saddle.

Raúl turned his back and stalked to the edge of the river, staring out at the rushing water.

Aurora dismounted and walked toward him. He didn't turn, but she felt he knew. He bent, picked up a stone, and hurled it out to the middle of the current. She closed the gap and stood beside him.

He didn't look at her. "I'm remembering, Aurora. Doomed, it seems, to memories and fantasies." His voice was hoarse. "I warn you, I've been drinking and my thoughts are not ones you want to share."

"Why are you drinking so early in the day, Raúl?"

"Iván can remove liquor from the *comedor* and even my room, but he can't remove my need—or my source. He only thinks he's in charge." Raúl glanced her way. "You need to go. My self-control whenever you're near me is incomplete and right now, it's stretched very thin. Go!"

"Raúl, don't fight this battle alone. Please, let me

stay and talk to you. I believe it may help."

He turned to her with such a blaze of passion in his eyes that Aurora almost fled, but she forced herself to stand her ground.

"You once told me not to pray for you, but I do," she said. "I pray for you often. I pray that you and I can come to understand one another."

He closed his eyes. "I understand you and you know what I want, Aurora. I love you in a way I've never experienced." He stepped nearer. She could smell liquor on his breath as his gaze probed hers, hot and angry.

"Do you have with Iván what you deny me, Aurora? Are you lovers?"

"No, Raúl. Iván is married and neither of us will breach the bond."

He continued his burning scrutiny. "Every morning, my first thought is of your rejection. It hurts, Aurora. I don't believe I can give you up to another man, even if that man is Iván." His hand closed around her arm.

"Raúl, you're forever thinking about what you want from me, but do you ever give thought to what I need from you?"

His astonishment was plain.

"Have you ever wondered how it feels for me, a woman facing your intensity? You're not a man who hides from truth. I believe you need to know. Will you listen now?"

Aurora took his hand from her arm and tugged. "Walk with me, Raúl." They took a few steps. "You say I've rejected you, but it's the other way around. You've been rejecting me from the minute you first saw me."

"I wanted more of you the minute I saw you."

She had his attention. "You refuse to see and hear the real me. You trivialize me."

His jaw went slack. "That's ridiculous—"

"Listen to me. The woman you think you're in love with does not exist. You created her in your own mind. You never gave me a chance to show you who I really am."

"If I could only convince you how seriously—"

Time to break that vein of thought. "Will you try to see the real me? You say you understand women. Let me talk honestly. I need answers and only you can help me."

He scowled. "I detest searching the soul."

"Of course. You're a man." She rolled her eyes. The hint of a smile touched his lips.

"I need a friend, Raúl. One who understands the part of my story I've never heard." She didn't try to hide the tears that welled up.

"Aurora." He whispered the word. He cupped her chin and drew her toward him. "There's a saying: 'A woman is a sometime thing.' I must agree. You are as variable in mood and unpredictable in movement as that river over there."

His manly scent filled her nostrils. He was possibly the most handsome man she'd ever seen. Intelligent. Strong. Expressive. Surely God had in mind a woman to appreciate all the fine attributes embodied in Raúl de Montaraz, but she was not that woman. Her heart was taken.

"At times you're a torrent in my soul, Aurora, and at others a trickle. I think there are dangerous currents and quicksands in you that can swallow a man. Still I seem to be unwilling to avoid the depth of your hold on me." He released her. "I'll listen, Aurora. I promise nothing, but talk to me."

Nineteen

Aurora pulled Raúl along the river path. "What was he like? Our father, Don León?"

"Why do you care what kind of man he was? Why not take your inheritance and leave? Leave this family and our problems and go wherever you wish. You're a wealthy woman because of León de Montaraz."

Raúl was clever, trying to control the situation, but Aurora meant to have some answers.

"I need to know of him. He's central to my story and he's hidden from me. Please, Raúl."

He stared ahead, walked for another few seconds, and stopped to face her. "Iván was the only son he loved. Yet I'm not sure whether Father loved Iván or what he believed he could achieve through him. I never felt loved by my father. He was proud of my appearance. Called me his most handsome son. Extolled my skill with a lariat. But I knew he didn't love me."

"You're very handsome and a wizard with a lariat, but why do you believe he didn't love you?"

"*Yo era su pollo baile.*" His voice was bitter.

"You were his dancing chicken? What do you mean? I've never heard such an expression."

"The performer to be trotted out and put through his paces. He could exhibit me to his friends as his handsome, wayward son. The antithesis of Iván. He encouraged my *machismo*. Pride, but no love. That was the father I knew."

The pain still showed. She could visualize the years of yearning for a father's real love, a love like Papá's.

"'Handsome men should enjoy themselves before they settle into marriage,' he said. He stretched his pleasure farther than that, yet I believe he cared for my mother. I'm not sure he understood love."

Did Raúl? Did he understand sacrificial love as Iván did?

They started to walk again. After a few steps, Aurora said, "But why do you believe he cared for Iván more than you?"

"Father invested himself in Iván. They spent hours riding together or closeted in the library. He perfected his favorite's horsemanship and swordsmanship while the rest of us waited on the sidelines. Iván was a natural with the court sword, being the fearless soul he is. It was he who taught us as he learned."

Duty to his brothers, always, but Raúl cannot see. He felt excluded.

Raúl stopped again. "As I think back on it, it seems their relationship was a competition. Iván determined to please Father, yet always seeking to better him. Only Iván succeeded in becoming a better swordsman and horseman than Father."

Insightful. A competition. She had discovered

the real man inside Raúl. He was talking to her, not posturing as the disappointed lover.

"And Justo, did he feel loved by your father?"

"No, Aurora. Elías had Iván, and Justo was close to our mother. I had neither. Three of us, though unrelated, were chosen at one time. Iván was eight when we were adopted, I was three, and Justo was an infant. Elías was adopted later."

"And your mother?"

"She was kind, but her attention had to be for the youngest. I don't think either of my younger brothers missed Father's love as I did."

An unusual admission for a proud man. Aurora felt closer to Raúl than she'd ever been.

His lips formed a wry smile. "Finding out about you was a shock for all of us."

"You were a shock for me, as well."

His face hardened. "That Father wanted you, an illegitimate child, to share in everything was a bitter pill. You shared his heart because you shared his blood. One more proof he cared more about his precious lineage than he did about me."

The beautiful little boy who ached for his father's love. If only she could comfort him, but she didn't dare hug him. The boy had become a man.

"You're wrong about not taking you seriously, Aurora. The moment I saw you—the first time I heard you speak—I took you seriously. You've affected me as no woman has ever done." He stepped toward her.

That again. She searched his face. "I believe you're afraid of me—the real me. You called me a dangerously beautiful woman. You fear I can reach a part of you that you keep hidden. We need to speak of that."

He shook his head, obviously at sea. "What?" The conversation had veered into channels he hadn't foreseen.

"It's far easier to hold onto your fantasy than to seek to know me, Raúl. You're afraid I may understand you and love you in a way you've never been loved."

He shook his head again. "Don't tell a man he's afraid, Aurora. You may get a reaction you won't like."

"I will love you. I'll love you the way God loves you. The real you. The lonely girl who lost her family far too early can understand the handsome boy who felt he never really had one."

He smiled, the dimples deep. "Well and good, but there's much more to a relationship with a man. You seem unaware of your physical effect on men. *Querida,* you could enslave me with your beauty alone. I'd be unable to resist you."

"It's not enough, and you know it. You would soon tire of my constant demand for soul-searching."

Raúl rolled his eyes, his lips a thin line. "No—"

"Please hear me. I need a small life. One dedicated to pleasing God. He has first place in my life, and until you know Him as I do, you'd find me frustrating. I follow God's leading, not because I have to, but because I want to. It's my fulfillment."

Raúl's face darkened and he shook his head.

"You want to lead a large life filled with excitement. You need adventure and challenge. I think you see me as a challenge, rather than loving me for who I am. We're opposites. We can learn from one another, but we're not suited to live with each other."

"I can't believe that's true, Aurora." Despite his objection Raúl's gaze had become thoughtful. He turned his eyes toward the river. Aurora waited until she had his attention once more.

"I think you realize I'm not the woman for you. That's why you try so hard to keep me in my place by talking about my beauty and your sexual prowess. What you feel for me is not love and I do not fear you, Raúl, because I see inside you to the truly honorable man you are."

"Honorable man?" He threw up his hands. "What a deliberate dash of cold water! Sexual prowess? What would you know of that? Woman, you are—" He glared at her and then slowly the corners of his mouth lifted and he laughed, the first she had heard from him in many weeks.

She laughed with him.

Raúl shook his head. "So my sobriquet is to be 'An Honorable Man.' Aurora, Aurora."

Thank you, Holy Father. Laughter is a beginning.

"A witty woman is even more interesting than a rich or a beautiful one. To find one that is all three—"

"Raúl, I'm serious. I see you among the most honorable of men. You've been loyal to Iván even though you believe he kept you from receiving the love and attention you deserved from your father. You work diligently for this ranch and the well-being of your brothers and employees. You offer love to the daughter of the man you believe wronged you. Yes, you are an honorable man."

His smile slipped and his brow furrowed. She mustn't lose him now.

"Raúl Francisco de Montaraz, I want you for my brother and my friend. We can learn from one another. There's much more to me than my face and my body. When you learn more of me, my attraction will disappear."

Aurora grinned and Raúl returned the smile. A little of the old deviltry gleamed in his brown eyes. "We'll see. I'm a determined man."

"I believe God has put us together for a reason. You'll learn to like me and I'll learn to love you—*honorably*." She stressed the last word and smiled up at him.

He growled, "An honorable man. I believe you overestimate me, Aurora."

Aurora allowed her smile to fade and peered up at him. "You also have a Father who loves you. A heavenly One. He loves you just as you are—not because you're handsome or capable or for what you can do for Him. You're not His dancing chicken."

Raúl said nothing. His gaze was no longer angry, but he looked confused.

Aurora's nod was slow and emphatic. She smiled again. "I must go. Jocasta will be looking for me; but we'll talk again. I'll always tell you truth. God has a plan for you and He'll accomplish much through you."

Raúl made no move to stop her. He steadied her as she mounted and waved as she rode away.

Twenty

In the late evening, Aurora and Iván strolled through the garden. Jocasta tussled with her new puppy, shrieking as he covered her face with kisses.

"I saw Raúl in the cove today and had a long talk with him. I think he has forgiven me."

Iván's jaw tightened, and his black eyes shrouded. "Raúl may not be a safe contact when he has been drinking. He feels strongly about you."

Oh, Iván someone had to try to reach him. It should have been you.

"But things still aren't right. Didn't you see how aloof he was during dinner? Respectful and sober, but not himself. Even Justo and Jocasta failed to raise his spirits. He was present, but not *there*."

"He's trying to come to terms with the situation. He's never failed with a woman before you." Iván knelt to join Jocasta and the puppy.

Aurora knelt beside him and touched his arm. "He's waiting for you to make the first move, Iván. He needs you."

"We'll see. Perhaps there will be opportunity now that he is sober."

Aurora saw no breakthrough in the following weeks. Raúl's eyes, almost as inscrutable as Iván's, were often on Aurora or Iván. He had little to say to either. Still brooding.

Why didn't Iván reach out? The other brothers looked on as helplessly as Aurora. Did Iván not know what to say? Or did he know his brother on a level she could not understand?

One morning she confronted Justo. "Can you do anything to help Raúl? He's not himself. It worries me."

He said, "I see it, also. He says nothing is wrong, but he takes unnecessary risks at work. Ropes a bull and doesn't wait for another vaquero to help him. It's as if he dares fate."

A month slid by. The yearning she read on Raúl's face in unguarded moments brought an ache to her throat. If only she could help him find solace; but he would not allow her to speak of spiritual matters.

Aurora took heart when Pía arrived for a two-day visit. Aurora waited at dinner the first night for him to blossom as he had before in Pía's company, but she saw no spark.

Justo was clearly smitten. He shone in dinner conversation and at the end of the meal said, "Señorita Pía, will you take a walk with me through the garden? I want you to see how well I have recovered." She agreed.

The next morning it was the offer of a ride, but Pía declined and Aurora's hopes sagged. She wanted for Pía what she would never have for herself—a marriage like Mamá's and Papá's. Either man would be a fitting mate, but Pía spoke only of her calling.

"So many times, sister, I'm able to share the welcome gospel of God's love with the ill before they die. Souls seem to open in the moments before death. Another gift of God's grace, I'm certain. One last chance to grasp His love and join Him forever."

Weeks passed. One summer day Genevra, Pía's assistant, came with distressing news. "*El gran dolor*. The great ache," Genevra said. "It is all around us. Muscle pain and blinding headaches are common among the ill, and fever so high it kills."

Aurora's hand covered her mouth. Mamá said the illness had taken the lives of both her parents in the same week. Pía had made a study of the mysterious disease. She said fifty years ago Italians began calling the malady *influenza.* They believed unfavorable astrology influenced the disease.

"The stars aren't involved," she'd said. "I believe it somehow travels from one person to another, but most doctors do not agree with me."

From perfect health, within a matter of hours, high fever dehydrated the afflicted. Their hearts and lungs were stressed by a wracking cough. Worse, a black depression of spirit accompanied the illness, causing victims to neglect their recovery. They wanted only to sleep, and would not drink or eat enough to maintain bodily functions.

Genevra said, "Pía sent me to check on all of you and to ask for supplies. The disease is spreading fast. The sick are urged to stay in their homes, although we are hard pressed to treat them. If both parents fall ill, their children are crowded into dormitories typically reserved for the unmarried. Even young, strong adults are victims."

Aurora sent Jorge for Iván. "How can we help?" she asked after he'd heard the nurse's story.

"Let Genevra requisition whatever she needs. I'll send a wagon every day. There is always extra soup and bread in the kitchens. Sofía is accustomed to feeding the sick."

In a matter of hours, Raúl and Justo accompanied Genevra back to the mission with cauldrons of soup and other provisions. It became a daily trip. Iván persuaded Aurora not to accompany them. "Pía will send for you if you're needed. We need you here."

She was reduced to questions each time they returned. Day after day, they reported Pía and Fray Peralta were standing strong, despite the continued spread of influenza.

At the end of the week, Iván summoned her to the library. He sat behind his desk, his long fingers steepled above a grim mouth. He shook his head, and her knees turned to jelly.

"Is it Pía?"

"No. My wife is ill. I must move into her quarters to care for her. I can't allow Lucera's usual caretakers to remain. They're no longer young people."

"You're not prepared to care for a sick woman. I'll go with you."

"No, Aurora, you're needed here. Catalina, Lucera's cook, has a brother who became ill at the mission. He went to his sister. Now both she and Lucera are sick. I must go." His expression brooked no argument. "Explain to Jocasta in some fashion. My brothers will have to manage without me. It could not be at a worse time, but my duty is clear."

"You cannot possibly care for three seriously ill people alone, Iván, what with meals, laundry, and bedside vigils. You'll have no time for rest and you'll sicken with them. I have experience from the mission hospital treating this illness."

His face darkened. "I will not allow you to place yourself in danger, *querida*. I'll manage alone. Everyone who is near this illness seems to be at risk." He stood up. The discussion was over.

Aurora took a deep breath. He wouldn't like what she was about to say. "Luisa and María will watch over Jocasta. She is very adult for a five-year-old. I'll explain to her that you and I will be caring for sick people in another place on the ranch. She'll understand."

His brows drew together and his eyes frosted. "Aurora, this is no time for your stubborn—"

"I must either go with you or on my own. It's the right thing, and you know it. Please, Iván. Let me gather items we'll need."

He raked a hand through his hair. "Jocasta needs you. You must think of her. You have become her touchstone."

"I always think of her. She's forever on my mind and in my heart, just as you are. She'll be safe in God's hands and in the care of her loving uncles while you and I see to the needs of truly helpless souls. You know I'm right."

Iván came around the desk and took her face between his hands. "I have a premonition of danger. This illness has claimed many lives already."

She stared up at him. "If you won't trust me, trust God. I am going with you."

He sighed and shook his head. "Can you be ready within the hour?"

"I'll explain to Jocasta and gather what we need from the medical storeroom and the kitchens. María will help me. Sofía has considerable skill in nursing. She can keep an eye on things here in the great house should anyone fall ill. Pía would come in a minute for Jocasta or your brothers." She pressed his fingers and turned toward the door.

Iván said to her departing back, "Why is it I can control the workings of this ranch and the actions of many men, only to find myself helpless before one small woman?"

They left the carriages for use in case of emergency. Both Corazón and Diego carried a hefty pack of supplies tied behind their saddles. A ride of a few miles found them in the stable yard of a small house tucked into a canyon several miles from Casa de Montaraz. A tall wall surrounded it.

Aurora stood before the chained and locked gate separating her—an interloper—from Iván's wife. Inside was a woman who commanded Iván's allegiance. The rightful mate to the man Aurora loved. Her hands trembled.

She must face a woman of uncertain mental stability, a patient sure to resist assistance from a stranger. If Iván was correct in assessing Lucera's mental condition, she would welcome death. She might want to take one or both of them to the grave with her, just as she had tried to kill Jocasta.

Iván's long fingers fumbled a minute with the gate's lock and Aurora took a step back. How would she react to this woman? She knew Iván's love in a manner Aurora never would. Their lovemaking produced a beautiful child, an experience forever denied Iván and Aurora.

Holy Father, please help me to see Lucera as You do, worthy of my best. Into Your hands, Father. Into Your hands.

Near the rear door to Lucera's house stood a stone-encased well and the entrance to an ice cellar. Walkways meandered through the yard beside trees and flowers. Was Lucera aware of the beauty Iván had created for her? Could she appreciate the care of a man who remained devoted, even after she tried to kill their child?

"*Patrón*," said the aging Indian woman who greeted Iván in the kitchen. She looked as tired as the elderly man who stood behind her. "Doña Lucera fell ill last night. Catalina is very ill and her brother, Eufamio, is dying. My husband brought fresh water and I gave them all broth and water this morning. None of them took much, Eufamio only two sips of water. A beef broth simmers on the fire—" Her voice faded away.

"You've done well, Rosario. Now take your husband and go to your daughter's house. It's my responsibility to care for my wife and the other two. I have a nurse to help me. Please pray for us."

Aurora examined supplies in the kitchen: a basket of Spanish oranges, a fresh supply of water, and the broth. She began unpacking some of Pía's medicinal herbs and remedies.

"Iván, will you please fill this large cauldron

with water and hang it over the fire? Pía believes steam vapors relieve coughing and difficult breathing."

He filled the big kettle and built up the fire, looking relieved to be of use. When he stood, Aurora read argument in the black eyes beneath his drawn brows. He'd had time to think.

She kept her voice confident. "Pía says to rinse everything used by the patient in boiling water. She cautions anyone caring for the ill to wash hands and bathe frequently. She believes cleanliness is essential in keeping disease from spreading. We'll need to keep this cauldron boiling."

"The problem is mine, Aurora. It's unwise for you to stay. I'll send for Sofía. She has experience nursing the ill. You can return to Jocasta."

"The problem is ours, Iván. I won't leave you. You would not allow Sofía to look after you. If you don't take proper care of yourself, you'll be next to sicken."

Iván sighed. "I have no idea where to begin, Aurora, but I'll do everything you tell me. Do not allow me to be as useless as I feel right now."

"We'll work together and God will direct us. Please pray with me." They went to their knees.

After asking God's guidance and blessing, Iván went to Lucera while Aurora finished laying out supplies. She steeled herself at his return to ask, "Will you take me to your wife?"

Lucera de Montaraz lay in a canopied bed in a room near the front of the house. Two large windows flooded light into the space, and Aurora took advantage of it to examine the sleeping woman.

Lucera's hair, matted and damp, was darker than Jocasta's. It must have once showed the same rich vitality, but not Jocasta's springy curls. Her facial features were similar to her daughter's, the same rosebud mouth and sweeping brow, but Jocasta's skin tone and hair were much lighter than either of her parents.

Aurora laid her hand on the woman's forehead, dismayed by the heat radiating from it. Lucera's black eyes snapped open and she seized the hand, squinting against the light.

Before Iván could speak, Lucera cried out, "Mariana, oh, Mariana! You've come! Or have I gone to you? Are we in heaven—or in hell? Surely heaven if you're here." Tears streamed down her cheeks as she gripped Aurora's hand. "I thought you forever gone from me but now you are here. Please, Sister, do not leave me again."

Iván glanced at Aurora. "We came to help you get well, Lucera. We'll stay with you until you're strong."

She kept her eyes riveted on Aurora. "Mariana, you've come."

"Iván and I will help you, but you must cooperate with your healing. This illness is a serious one. Please do everything we say." Aurora pushed Lucera's hair from her face. "Iván will bring broth for you and a glass of fresh water. You must drink it all."

A frown creased Lucera's brow. "You were always bossy, but somehow I never minded you telling me what to do. I know you love me as Mother and Father never did. I'll do what you say. I never want to displease you in the way I did our parents. They cannot forgive me." Her fevered eyes looked haunted.

Twenty-One

Aurora looked at Iván. What should she do? She would not lie. God always wanted truth. She patted Lucera's hand and chose her words carefully.

"God assures us in His Word that nothing is ever so bad it cannot be forgiven. He forgives us as soon as we ask. God loves you, even more than your sister Mariana." She smiled. "I'll bring your hair brush and help you wash your face and hands."

Iván came in a bowl of broth. After propping Lucera with extra pillows Aurora took from a linen press, he began spooning it to the reluctant woman.

Aurora pulled draperies across the windows, realizing the room's brightness must be worsening the headache that accompanied the dread illness. Pía said it killed thousands of people in Spain, France, and Italy in the last century, and then abated as mysteriously as it had spread.

In the kitchen Aurora squeezed oranges to fill a glass with juice and measured out a careful dose of quinine into another, diluting it with water. Pía made quinine from the pulverized bark of the cinchona tree, saying the medication alleviated lung congestion. Aurora stirred a small amount of the sleep-producing herb valerian into the juice.

Lucera grimaced at the bitter quinine. She quickly washed it down with orange juice. When she slept again, Aurora and Iván washed their hands in a steaming basin. "Pía insists on extreme cleanliness. She believes it keeps down the spread of infection."

"I won't argue with her medical wisdom. Think of what she did for Justo."

They went to examine Catalina and Eufamio. Both were very ill.

"The young man is dying, Iván. He probably won't live through the night. His lungs have filled, and his fever has reached unbearable levels. Thankfully, he's unconscious and will not suffer more than he has already." She wiped his heated face with a moist cloth. "Is there ice in the cellar?"

"I'll check. Raúl can bring more. He wanted to come with us, but I convinced him he can be more helpful as liaison."

Catalina's brother died before dawn, while she lay too ill to speak. Later Aurora watched Iván and Raúl through a kitchen window. The men unloaded packs of food and blocks of ice from a cart before beginning the dreaded chore of the morning.

"You must return to the *casa principal,* Aurora. I'll stay in your place," Raúl said.

"I'm of more use here. Someone must cook and see to chores. I can do that more effectively than you, whereas I cannot help Justo and Elías haul supplies to the mission."

He finally gave up and helped Iván carry Eufamio's blanket-covered body through the front door and place their sad burden into the wagon.

"Lord, please bring these brothers together in You," Aurora whispered as she watched Raúl lock the gate behind him.

Twenty-Two

Aurora returned to Lucera's room. Her heart lifted when Lucera said, "Mariana." Her voice was weak, but she was still able to speak.

Iván brought broth as Aurora lifted the woman's head and insisted she drink some juice. Lucera whispered, "Who is that man? Please send him away."

"This is Iván, your husband. He wants to help. He has broth for you. Please eat as much as you can. You'll feel stronger."

Iván fed Lucera several times a day as Aurora went about other tasks. Sometimes he read to her, or sat beside the bed in silence as she slept.

What were his thoughts? What did he feel for Lucera? His persistent presence testified to his caring. Was it a sense of duty that impelled him—or a renewed hope for the mother of his child? Lucera was a beautiful woman. Iván must have felt more than he'd disclosed.

Each day's labor ended in hours of nightly routines. At the end of five stressful days, Catalina's condition was improving, but Lucera deteriorated before their eyes. Breathing became increasingly difficult for her. Aurora realized her lungs were filling.

Liberal doses of quinine failed to divert the direction of the disease. Fever spiked to dangerous levels and Lucera's rigid body shook with chills. Steam baths brought little relief. Aurora soothed her with cool cloths and encouraged her to swallow icy liquids.

Iván hovered near, pacing and raking a hand through his mane. On the sixth night, an especially bad one, Lucera's cough ceased around midnight and she slipped into a peaceful nap. Iván went to Catalina and Aurora nodded off in a chair at Lucera's bedside. After an hour, Aurora felt her hands caught in a strong grip.

Lucera sat up without help and spoke without the usual gasping. "Let me die! You know what I did. I betrayed all of you, but I've been punished enough, Mariana."

"Don't talk this way. You're cooler to my touch. I believe the fever is abating. You'll live, Lucera."

"I don't want to live in this hell I made. I gave myself to a man other than the one Father chose, then married a man I could not love. I grew to hate him and killed my child. Let me go to the hell God has prepared for me. It cannot be worse than the one I have fashioned for myself."

Lucera appeared more rational than she had been in all the days Aurora had been with her. Had the fever somehow restored her mind? Perhaps it burned away the insanity and depression. Aurora prayed for it to be so.

Iván deserved a wife who could respond, and Jocasta would be thrilled to have a mother. The thought surprised Aurora with its rightness. She could at long last give Iván into the hands of God. She could face a future without him. Whatever God willed would bring fulfillment. His plan for her life's journey was all she'd ever need.

"Jocasta is not dead, Lucera. You child lives! A beautiful, intelligent little girl who will be thrilled to know her mother. Live for her, Lucera. Live that you may know your daughter."

"What are you saying, Mariana? Trying to soothe me with a lie? I threw her down the steps. She cannot be alive." Lucera's gaze searched Aurora's and her grip grew painful. "Do not lie to me, *hermana*."

"Never, Lucera. Jocasta is a healthy child, beloved by all in the house, most of all by her father. God wants to reunite you three as a family and give you a life with Him. Forgiven, and restored to your proper place. Please listen to me."

"Now I know you lie, Mariana. You know Iván is not Jocasta's father." Lucera's face twisted. "You know I was pregnant with Rodolfo's child before I married Iván. He didn't know, but you did. That's why you allowed yourself to die of the illness you fought so bravely for years."

She sobbed and pushed Aurora away. "You could not live with my deceit. You chose to die rather than witness my shame. You knew Mother and Father could never forgive me, and you know God cannot forgive sins such as mine."

Aurora stared at her. A parallel to her own story! A man rearing an illegitimate child as his own. Another delusion, or was Lucera reliving her true past? It could explain why she tried to kill her infant, a bastard child foisted on an unsuspecting bridegroom.

I must find words. She had to convince Lucera that no matter how large and ugly her sin, God had forgiven her—and so had Iván.

"Iván counts the child his own, Lucera. He loves her more than he loves himself. No one holds you in condemnation. For the very reasons of which you speak, our Savior died. Jesus died so the sins of all could die with Him and we can live free. You know this. Please trust God now. Tell Him you want forgiveness."

Lucera's expression changed. She appeared to consider Aurora's words. "Does my daughter truly live? Oh, I want to believe that! I need to believe it. She didn't deserve to die—I should have. Why did I not throw myself down those steps? I don't understand, but I need to believe." Tears ran down her cheeks.

"You need to believe because it's true, Lucera. I'm going to leave you now and send Iván to tell you that he has forgiven you and how much he loves Jocasta. She is his life. He devotes himself to her, and he has never given up hope you will be well and strong again, restored to what you're meant to have. He has visited you often during your illness and has sought the best of care for you. I'll ask him to come now. Let him hear your confession."

Aurora did not speak to Iván of what Lucera told her, only that she was rational and needed to see him. He had been napping at Catalina's bedside in a large chair that Aurora had sought to make more comfortable with plumped pillows and a footstool. She watched his rise, slow and painful. She laid a hand to his forehead.

"Iván, you have a fever. Please wait before you go to Lucera. I'm going to bring quinine and some of Pía's cough remedy."

After Iván swallowed the medications, he went to Lucera's room and Aurora took his place beside Catalina, who was awake. Aurora brought broth for her patient and a glass of orange juice for herself. After she coaxed a little soup and a sleeping potion down Catalina, Aurora settled in the chair, sipping her juice and praying between bouts of fitful sleep.

Once she looked in on Lucera, who appeared to be sleeping peacefully. Iván held her hand as he dozed in a chair at her bedside. Aurora finally drifted off into a deep sleep and was awakened in the first light of dawn by Catalina's weak voice.

"Nurse, how long have I been ill? What of Eufamio, my brother?" Catalina's eyes were clear and she was cool to Aurora's touch. She would recover.

Aurora found words to give Catalina the sad news of her brother's death, and the two women cried together for several minutes.

"He was a good man," Catalina said. "God will receive him."

"I'll bring you something to eat," Aurora said.

Just outside the doorway she bumped into Iván. His fever-flushed face carried a haunted expression.

"Lucera is gone. Her suffering is finished." His eyes held the shock of his news.

Aurora staggered. "It cannot be, Iván. She was strong and rational only hours ago, in complete command of her faculties. She sat up without help. Her grip on my hands was strong—her fever less. She knew Jocasta lived. She wanted to see her daughter and you. She cannot be gone. Not now when there was such hope. Oh, Iván!"

Aurora threw herself into his arms and he held

her close. They sought comfort from the irony of an illness that restored Lucera to her world and then snatched it from her. Aurora wept.

Iván whispered into her hair. "You did all you could, little one. She understood she was forgiven because of you. You brought her God's peace. He used you, Aurora."

She raised her face to his. Tears rolled down his cheeks. "All I can do now is to make her tomb within sight and sound of the sea—her request in sane times. She said her troubled soul could lie beside a restless ocean, but I believe it's now a soul at peace."

Aurora at last persuaded Iván to lie on a couch near the fireplace of the living room. "You must, Iván. Your fever is rising." At his side, she prayed and dozed fitfully until she heard Raúl's voice in the kitchen. Thank God! He could accomplish Lucera's burial.

When he returned, Raúl insisted upon staying with Aurora to help her with Iván. Justo became the link to the main house, bringing daily news and provisions. Within four days, Raúl threatened to tie a stubborn Aurora into the bed recently vacated by Catalina. He had carried her from Iván's bedside, her struggles weakened by fever and coughing. He sent for Pía.

Raúl watched Pía assume control, brushing aside Aurora's protests with calm authority. Aurora remained in bed, finally admitting she was too weak to be of help. Pía was a comforting presence, although she did not try to hide the gravity of Iván's illness. It was apparent to Raúl that she believed Iván was losing the battle.

Lucera's untimely death freed Iván to build a

life with Aurora, but would he survive to claim it? Did Raúl want him to? He'd thought, more than once, of advantages to Iván's death—Aurora and the ranch, possibly his. Could thoughts influence reality? Had he cursed his brother with malevolent ideas? Some people believed in the power of malediction.

Raul could not force his mind from a circuitous pattern of uncertainty and, he at last recognized, regret. He'd recognized Iván's efforts for the family, but he'd resented the control of a brother who seemed to fall naturally into the role of authority.

I need to talk to Aurora, but she's too ill.

Guilt goaded him. He threw himself into an effort to bring healing to a brother he resented. He and Pía were at Iván's bedside one evening, trying to get some liquids into him when she looked up, a strange expression on her face.

"Raúl, will you go now to Aurora and do what you can for her? I will come after I have finished medicating Iván."

Raúl found Aurora locked in a rigorous chill, shaking so hard he feared she might hurt herself. He stood a moment, undecided. Pulling off his boots, he climbed into bed beside her. Tugging her against him, he rubbed her back and arms. He kissed her hair, and pleaded with her.

"Aurora, don't die. Please do not die. Jocasta needs you; I need you." He finally added, "Iván needs you. Please get well. I love you so much." Could he give her up to Iván?

Aurora's eyes were tightly closed and her teeth chattered in helpless spasms. Her skin felt hot and dry to his touch. Fear twisted his gut. She looked so small and helpless. He sought to warm her quaking body with his.

She's lost weight and had none to spare. A fine woman. Always wanted what was good for me. And I only to take from her.

Why had he not appreciated her as he should? He'd closed his mind to her pleading for his very soul. Shame and remorse welled up. His throat constricted as he continued to beg. "I'll change, Aurora. I'll be the man you want me to be, the brother you need. I promise, *querida*, if you'll just get well. Please do not die."

Tears poured down his cheeks and he buried his face in her hair, that once-glorious mane now glued to her head with perspiration. The spasms continued. He continued to plead and to promise a new future for her and for himself. Her tremors abated. He opened his eyes and looked into the unsmiling face of Pía, who stood at the foot of the bed.

Raúl felt sick. What must she think, finding him in Aurora's bed, holding her as he was?

"Pía, please do not misunderst—"

"Of course not. I know why you are in Aurora's bed. I've done the same for a patient when a chill would not subside. It's the reaction of a natural healer. I watched you with Justo and with Iván. You have a sense of a sick person's needs. I know because I have the same ability. It's one given to some by God for His purposes."

Raúl realized his jaw had gone slack. "I've never thought of myself as a healer, nor as a man of particular understanding. No one has ever said such a thing to me."

"When Aurora's chill eases, I'll need you with me

for Iván." She touched her forehead. "A few minutes ago I sent you away, thinking it was the end, but he's still with us. I want to try a cooling bath to reduce the fever. It has reached dangerous levels and he may go into convulsions. Strange, isn't it? The same fever that causes chills comes in waves of heat that can kill the brain." She turned away.

"Thank you, Pía, for believing me. I feared—"

"That I might think you would take advantage of Aurora? Raúl, I know you would never do anything to harm Aurora. You are an honorable man."

Raúl thought for a hysterical moment he might laugh. "I've heard similar words from Aurora."

"Of course you have. She can see into your heart just as I can. She has never said much about you brothers, other than what honorable men you are." She left to return to Iván.

As soon as Raúl was able to leave Aurora, he and Pía administered a cooling bath and changed Iván's nightshirt and bed linens. In the kitchen Raúl ladled out a basin of boiling water, into which Pía measured aromatic herbs and slivers of tree bark from the array of healing agents on one of the tables.

Raúl and Pía tugged Iván into position. He lay face down across the bed, his head hanging beyond.

Pía said, "Get astraddle his back and hold Iván's head over the basin. I'll arrange towels to form a tent."

Raúl's arms went rigid with the effort of holding his brother's head and shoulders. Pía encouraged Iván to inhale the herb-laden steam.

When the coughing became intense, she directed, "Pound his back to free up congestion."

At last they finished and Iván was allowed to lie

back, propped up by pillows. He looked very weak.

Pía said, "He is in the hands of the Father. I wish I could tell you he is improving, but I have no physical basis for hope. I've seen this illness strike down strong and able-bodied men. Iván will need all of his considerable strength to combat it."

"He must not die, Pía. We must try harder!"

She shook her head. "We can only pray harder. I believe Aurora's is a lighter case. Her chest is less congested than Iván's and her cough productive. I have hope for her." Pía's lovely face stared up at him in sympathy.

Raul refused to leave the Iván's bedside for two more days, despite Pía's admonitions about caring for himself. He talked to his unconscious brother, telling him of his new insights. He begged forgiveness, and promised better behavior and happier times. He even relinquished Aurora. Could Iván hear his words?

Twenty-Three

Two days later, Aurora sat propped by fluffy pillows as her sister puttered around the sickroom. Pía had become a beautiful woman. Today thick black braids wound like shadows around her head. Jocasta once said Pía reminded her of the small black butterflies winging gracefully about the garden. Pía did flit from chore to chore, as if her feet skimmed above the floor. Aurora had seen her arms outstretched like wings to comfort a sick person or to hug a child.

I've never seen Pía angry, but I have seen her vexed by resistance to good sense, and she is vexed right now.

Pía stood, hands on her hips after she finished tucking the coverlet. "Raúl will be the next one to fall ill if he doesn't listen to reason. I'm sending him to you, Aurora. He trusts you in a rare way, it seems."

Aurora's eyebrows rose. "I'm not so certain—" Her words were a weak murmur. Pía took no notice.

"Without rest and proper nutrition, he, too, will become ill. I take time to rest and eat. I maintain strict hygiene, and God keeps me safe. If I flaunted the wisdom He has given me, I would succumb."

"Send him to me, Pía. Perhaps I can talk some sense into him," Aurora whispered.

Raúl came into Aurora's room a half hour later. Pulling a chair to her bedside, he took her hand. His face looked drawn—haunted. Was he falling ill?

"You are going to live, Aurora, but Iván is dying. More than once I wished him dead and now he is dying. What am I going to do? I don't want him to die." Raúl's brown eyes shadowed with pain and he raked at his hair, very Iván-like.

Aurora squeezed his fingers with the strength she could muster. Words were impossible. Iván! She couldn't imagine him so ill that he could not recover. There must be hope.

"The fever rages on and he grows weaker by the hour," Raúl murmured. "Pía has done all she can. Her teas and the quinine are of no avail. Steam baths are useless." His gaze burned into hers. "I do not want him to die!"

"Of course you don't," Aurora whispered. She realized Raúl strained to hear her words. She had to make him understand. She motioned him closer. His grip on her hand had become painful. He was close to breaking.

She forced more strength into her voice. "Iván will die only if he has finished the work God has given him here on earth, Raúl. It is God who determines the hour and it will have nothing to do with your wish."

He sobbed and covered his eyes. She wanted to cry with him. Iván, her strong man, lay at death's door. The ache in her chest had little to do with the cough that still wracked her on occasion.

Raúl knelt and took her hand. "Aurora, will you pray for him? My soul is on its knees, but I have no words. Will you offer words I cannot find?" He looked like a man still recovering from a long illness, stressed and drained.

She nodded and reached for his other hand. His eyes were closed, but tears slipped down his cheeks. She whispered, "Into Your hands, Holy Father. We give our desires for Iván's healing and all of our weaknesses into Your hands."

Raúl's eyes snapped open. His gaze burned into Aurora's. "That's all? That is your only prayer for the man you love—my brother—who lies at death's door?"

"We are God's, Raúl. Iván, you, Pía, and I—we all belong to God. In His loving hands is where we need to be, and it is all we need. He does the perfect thing. We don't need to tell Him what to do."

Raúl bowed his head and cried as if he could never stop. Aurora stroked his hand. At last, he lifted his face. His expression had changed. Hope shone in his eyes.

"It's true, Aurora. God is our loving Father. I'm so glad that Iván is His and that I also belong to Him."

Aurora stroked his head, bowed again beneath her hand. "Yes, dearest Raúl, it's true."

He raised his head and stared at her as if he'd never seen her before. "All that you have ever said to me is true. I was wrong, Aurora. Wrong to try to take you from Iván. I finally recognize the rightness of the love you have for him and his for you. He is the man for you. I could never be worthy—"

"Nothing to do with your worthiness. You are an honorable man." Aurora mustered a smile.

He grinned and kissed her cheek. "I suppose I must accept the title. Pía insists on the same."

Within minutes, Raúl fell into an exhausted sleep with his head still on Aurora's bed. Pía came sometime later and moved him into a more comfortable position with his head back on a pillow in the deep chair. She placed a stool beneath his feet, removed his boots, and tucked a blanket around him. He did not wake.

She sat on the opposite side of Aurora's bed. Love brimmed in her gaze. "Iván is sleeping in God's hands, just as you prayed. I dare offer a word of hope. His breathing is improving."

"Oh, Pía. I'm so thankful. We praise You, Holy Father."

Pía nodded. "I listened, Aurora. I listened as you spoke to Raúl. I knew you could help him. I've always known I could count on you."

Aurora closed her eyes to hide the tears.

"We've shared so much," Pía continued. "Laughed more joyously and cried less miserably because we're sisters. All women should have a sister like you, Aurora."

"I cannot imagine life without you, *hermanita.*"

Pía shared a cheeky smile. "I'm thankful you came in obedience and that I followed you to this place. You led me to this ranch where God has revealed him to me—the strong man I need beside me for the rest of my life. I never expected such an outcome."

"Oh, Pía, have you decided that you love Justo, after all? I realized he was drawn to you, but I didn't recognize any response in you."

"Justo? I speak of Raúl."

Aurora stared at Pía. Why was she surprised?

They were perfect for each other.

"Raúl will go with me to Mexico City. He can apprentice to a fine doctor and we can continue to learn together of how to alleviate the suffering of the ill." Pía's smile was rapturous. "God will use Raúl's charisma and quick mind. We can improve the condition of many with his great fortune, and you and his brothers can share in our ministry. We will all be blessed."

Pía's words sounded right. Raúl was the vigorous mate she needed, and she was the woman of strength who would venture with him unafraid, willing to follow his lead in God's wisdom.

"Does Raúl know, Pía?"

"Not yet."

The two women laughed together as Raúl continued his sorely-needed rest, his handsome face looking once again boyish in sleep.

Within two days, Iván began to recover. At the end of a week, Aurora was moved into the same large room in a smaller bed during daylight hours.

From the doorway, Raúl said, "Putting you together means fewer trips for us. You can have brief intervals in chairs beside the window, while your pillows and bedding air in the sun, but bed rest is still the order of the day."

The words made sense. Relapse was a haunting possibility with influenza.

Raúl issued an order. "Aurora, see that Iván drinks everything we bring and takes his medications. He'll keep an eagle eye on you, but he may think his wisdom is greater than mine. You must help one another, but Pía and I will be near." He smiled them, and then down at Pía, who stood within the circle of his arm.

"You once wisely said to me, Aurora, that I wanted a large life, filled with adventure and success. Those words took root in my soul. I longed for such a life. I envied others who had found the lives they sought. I had no purpose until I found Pía. She has helped me find God's intention for my life and she is the woman to share it."

Iván said, "The right woman is God's blessing." His somber black gaze sought Aurora's.

Raúl added, "We'll supervise your recovery, but we have important plans to work out. You two may want to use some of your minutes in the same manner."

After Pía and Raúl left, Iván said, "Our lives have changed, Aurora. We can make new choices." He smiled that heart-quickening smile.

"Yes, Iván, we can, and I've been considering some of them." She winged a prayer and looked into his expectant face. "You can become the older brother Raúl has always needed. Admit to him how you've failed him all these years and welcome him to feast with you on the Father's love. The whole family can celebrate with him."

A frown furrowed Iván's brow. "What are you saying? How have I failed my brother? I have tried to do what was best. I protected him from his own folly on every possible occasion. Do you not understand?"

"*Sí, mi amor.* I know—but Raúl does not. You've not told him the reason behind your actions. He needs to hear your words. Unlike the elder brother in Jesus' parable, you must welcome him home. He doesn't understand you shouldered the demands of a prideful father who could never be satisfied. That you did it to spare your brothers."

Iván looked confused. She explained, "Raúl saw you and your father sharing a life that excluded him. He felt rejected, unworthy of either of you."

Iván shook his head. "I don't know what to say."

"You must find words to explain. Open yourself to him in a way you never have. Listen to his misunderstandings and answer his accusations in love. Sacrifice once more so he can become the man God intends him to be."

Aurora's legs quivered, but she was able to cross the space to Iván. He pulled her onto his lap and she stroked his hair.

"God wants that man for His purposes, Iván. You and I can be used to help Raúl find them. He and Pía will change the world in small but important ways, and we'll support them."

A quiet moment passed; then Iván said, "Perhaps I am too convinced of my own wisdom and vision at times. Help me to seek God's guidance, Aurora. I want complete honesty in my relationship with my brothers and with you."

His eyes worshiped her. She dreaded her next words, but the time had come. "Then why didn't you tell me that you did not father Jocasta? Why hide the fact, even after we came to a new understanding?"

The shutters closed. Iván's stare locked on Aurora's. A muscle along his jaw tightened. Had she gone too far? The silence thickened. He bowed his head.

"I do not dwell on the fact that I did not father Jocasta," he said. "A prideful man has a hard time admitting he has been duped. I didn't suspect Lucera's pregnancy when we were betrothed. Unlike your father, I would not have been capable of such generosity."

Tears stood in Aurora's eyes.

Iván continued, "It's no sacrifice to love Jocasta," he said. "She has always been God's gift to me. I'm sure your father felt the same."

Aurora's tears spilled and Iván wiped them away. He kissed her cheek. "Part of my early attachment may have been pity for an infant whose mother was incapable of loving her. But it quickly changed into wonder at the magnificence of the tiny bundle of life that was Jocasta. She wrapped herself so tightly around my heart that I think of her only as my own. She is my daughter, Aurora."

"I love her in the same way."

"I know, my love, I know."

The corner of Iván's mouth lifted. He held out a glass to Aurora. "Drink your juice. If we expect to manage our own lives soon, we must convince those two we are serious about recovery. Raúl enjoys his control over his older brother." He picked up his own glass and drained it.

Two months later, Pía and Raúl were married in the chapel of Rancho de Montaraz. Beside them were Iván and Aurora as attendants and Jocasta as flower girl. Aurora noticed Raúl's fervent gaze focused only on Pía.

Raúl had found the woman to complete his strong and passionate nature. They would take on accepted medical wisdom—argue with it, make new discoveries, travel, experiment, and learn. Pía's quiet confidence was a perfect balance to Raúl's emotional daring. She would direct his quick mind into new channels.

After Pía and Raúl were wed, they took their places as witnesses to the marriage of Iván and Aurora. Iván lifted the flower girl into his arms for the vows. Jocasta had asked to marry Aurora as her mother and Fray Peralta adjusted the ceremony to allow for her response.

"I do accept my beloved teacher and friend as my mother," her sweet little voice declared. "And I will obey her loving advice and that of my father always."

~

As Fray Peralta observed the couples, tears rose in his eyes. He would never tell Aurora of his own uncertainty when he asked her—a young woman caught up into a story she could not yet comprehend—to go to Rancho de Montaraz. He, too, had been unable to understand. He could only obey the Whisper that counseled him to send her.

I could not know the outcome. We followed Your lead one step at a time, Holy Father. The troubled soul of Lucera de Montaraz has been saved. The Good Shepherd sought her out, that lost, lonely one, using our obedience. Other consequences will follow. Great ones and small ones. You have a plan for all of the lusty brothers de Montaraz.

The End

Painting of San Carlos Borromeo de Monterey
(today known as Carlos Borromeo de Carmelo)
by Oriana Day
Courtesy California Missions Resource Center

Please visit Marilyn and Cheryl at
Inspired Women of the Southwest.
www.InspiredWomenoftheSW.com

Marilyn and Cheryl greatly appreciate all reader feedback! Would you consider leaving a brief review of this book on Amazon, Goodreads, or any other book review site? We thank you!

Made in the USA
Lexington, KY
26 November 2019